Praise for Puja Guha's work

Ahriman: The Spirit of Destruction

"Like Grisham and Clancy... this title shines among the genre simply though superb storytelling."

—Recommended by The US Review of Books
(Reviewed by Michael Radon)

"A classic nail biter – couldn't put the book down..."

—Reader

"A sophisticated globetrotting thriller, the best elements of Bourne Identity and Covert Affairs."

—Reader

The Confluence

Puja Guha

www.pujaguha.com
pujaguha@pujaguha.com

ISBN 978-0-9905930-1-0

THE CONFLUENCE

Puja Guha

Also by Puja Guha

Spy Thriller Suspense Series:

The Ahriman Legacy Book 1 – *Ahriman: The Spirit of Destruction*

Upcoming release 2016: The Ahriman Legacy Book 2

Contemporary Indian Family Drama / Women's Fiction:

The Confluence

THE CONFLUENCE

To every family's lost souls:
It is never too late to come home.

Foreword

This story begins in 2045 as Naina writes an elongated letter to her now grown son Nikhil that recounts the journey that led to his adoption.

Decades earlier, Naina stumbled upon information about the location of an aunt who disappeared when Naina was just a child. After her aunt's disappearance, Naina's family also lost complete contact with her beloved younger cousin, Nitu. Once Naina learned of her aunt's location, she realized it could be the first step to finding her cousin and she traveled to the Republic of East Africa to find her aunt.

As an author, I created this fictitious country based on my travels through a number of Middle Eastern and African countries. East Africa's capital city is Taisoun, and it encompasses what I found most interesting and captivating during my visits to many cities in the two regions. This fabricated country and city are composites of many existing locales, with the addition of a heaping spoonful of fiction to create a unique setting for the story.

In her letter, Naina describes both her physical and emotional journey as she travels between Taisoun and Calcutta. This journey changes her life forever, leading to Nikhil's adoption and, eventually, the need to write her story.

May 15, 2045 – Prologue: My promise

Memories. Some of them are as distant as the day they occurred, while others reside at the forefront of our minds. I'm not sure why this occurs. I spent three years studying biology in college when I was supposed to be premed, and I never found anyone able to successfully explain the operations of the human mind. My grandfather once told me that being able to forget was humanity's most important blessing. How else would we be able to forgive? How else could we move forward after experiencing egregious loss? Perhaps being able to forget enriches our existence. Some memories will always evoke certain emotions from our minds, hearts, and souls, but the bite that resonates can lessen over time. While I agree that being able to forget is important, every time I look at you, I have to disagree with him. There can be no disputing it—memory is humanity's most important blessing.

No matter how many years have passed, the first time I saw you still feels like yesterday. Nikhil, you were only three at the time, sitting on your haunches stacking Lego blocks onto the back of a large green toy truck. You were so meticulous and attentive to the last detail, even then. I should have known you would go on to become a civil engineer. Nothing else would have made sense.

We never told you about the circumstances that led to that meeting, or to your adoption. I can give you all kinds of excuses. Your father and I were worried about how much pain it might cause. We didn't want to confuse your ideas about your heritage. Mostly, we were just afraid. Afraid that you would think that we loved you less than your sister. Afraid that you might believe that you were not really our son. Afraid that you wouldn't know how to relate to your sister knowing that you are not blood siblings. Afraid that you would want to seek out your biological parents rather than continue to live in the home that we had built as a family.

When we finally told you that you were adopted, you didn't seem to be too surprised. Perhaps you saw the signs. They are everywhere if you know what to look for. We never did tell you about how your adoption came to be, though. We never told you that you and I do indeed share blood, just not as your parent. We never told you who your biological father was and how much he meant to me. Nikhil, we were always family, even before your adoption.

Last week I watched you march across that stage in a cap and gown to receive your PhD. When Kanika told us that you two were expecting, we could not have been more excited. But it made me realize that you are a grown man, and you deserve the truth, especially now. As you bring your own child into the world, you should know every detail I can tell you about your entire past. So here it is, in all of its pain and glory.

****

March, 2017 – When everything started

Dear Nikhil,

Your father proposed to me after we'd been living together in a small flat in Paris for a little over a year. I cried and we laughed, and then we toasted and danced with a group of our friends. After the initial excitement had worn off, we made plans for me to visit his family in New York. Dev had met my parents when they had visited Paris a number of times, but I had yet to meet his family.

I was so scared of the prospect of meeting your *Dida.* Dev maintained that I had nothing to worry about, that his mother would love me, but his background is so different from my own that I couldn't help being concerned. I'm sure that you've noticed the differences between our families for years now. He grew up in what I can only call a mansion in one of the wealthiest suburbs of New York City, while I grew up in cramped apartments around the world. Please don't mistake this for saying that I grew up poor. Far from it. I always had everything that I wanted and more. Your *Nanni* and *Nanu* are professionals who always earned a decent living, and I couldn't have more wonderful parents. There is of course, however, a huge difference between the middle class and the uppermost echelons of the upper class. I was never fully aware of that distinction until that first visit to your Dida and *Dadu*'s home. I hadn't even realized that there were families of Indian descent in the United States who had managed to amass such incredible wealth or political clout. I certainly hadn't processed what that would mean for me as I married into their family while your Dadu was a member of cabinet.

Dev and I had booked our tickets to New York, and my mom decided to join us on the trip as well from London. At the last minute, something urgent came up with Dev's business, so he stayed in Paris for a few extra days while Mom and I kept our trip dates. Without Dev, we didn't feel comfortable staying at his family's home, so we checked into a budget hotel about half an hour away.

I will preempt this part of the story by saying that I don't want to make your Dida out to be something that she isn't. She is a wonderful woman, and I have seen beautiful qualities in her since I formally joined her family. The prospect of joining her family, however, is something that she kept considerably guarded. I expected this to a degree, but the reality far surpassed what I had envisioned. My first encounters with her felt cold and filled with resentment. We eventually came to forgive each other and even warm to each other's company. She has always showered you with so much love, and I do not want to sour your vision of her. Like all of us, she has many flaws, but her good qualities drastically outweigh them. It just took me a while to stumble upon those good qualities.

The day after Mom and I checked into the hotel, Dev sent me an e-mail that his mother was expecting us at the house that afternoon. He wouldn't be able to arrive until the following day, but he wanted us to meet her as soon as possible, rather than waiting for his arrival. I was apprehensive, but I agreed. I wasn't sure how we should dress, so Mom suggested that we go for traditional Indian clothes. She had brought an old *lehenga* that she thought would fit me, along with a *sari* for herself.

That afternoon I donned the lehenga. It looked beautiful but made me feel like someone outside of myself. You've seen me wear it; it's your sister's favorite. The skirt is that gorgeous azure blue and the top piece has some intricate silver embroidery. I can't believe it's still considered fashionable today.

I must have stared at the mirror for an hour before Mom finally forced us into the car that your Dida had sent to the hotel. On the drive to their house, I felt as if I were heading to the guillotine dressed in my Sunday best.

The house in Westchester wouldn't seem like such a shock to you because you grew up spending time there. I want you to try to picture how it must have been for me. Just the driveway wraps around the property for at least a mile. When you finally get to the house, it resembles a colonial plantation more than a home. I still don't understand why on earth they wanted a house with that many bedrooms.

A butler opened the car doors for us and led us up the marble staircase and into the foyer. While we were waiting for your Dida to come down and greet us, I walked over to the hall bathroom. I almost gasped aloud when I saw the size. That bathroom must be over four hundred square feet—larger than our entire apartment in Paris.

Shortly after I emerged, your Dida finally came to greet us. She looked much as she does now, just with a little less gray hair. She walked straight and tall in a slim-cut maroon dress accessorized with a single strand of pearls. I kicked myself for letting Mom talk me into wearing traditional Indian dress, and I cursed silently at Dev for abandoning us to face this moment without him.

"I am Madam Ranjeeva. You must be Naina," I remember her saying while giving me a once-over with her eyes. From that moment on, Madam Ranjeeva is the only way I referred to your Dida back then, at least when neither she nor Dev were around.

"It's so nice to finally meet you, Auntie," I exclaimed.

"Follow me please." Her tone was icy, and my knees felt weak as I stood up. She turned without any further response and headed down the hallway.

I felt my purse vibrate and opened it hastily to glance at my phone for messages. There was a text from Dev. *"Did you meet her yet?"*

"Yes, just got here," I quickly typed so he would know that I'd received his text immediately.

Within seconds, Dev replied, *"Sorry can't be there."*

I sighed. *"It's okay. Just miss you."*

"Will be there in two days."

I fought a frown that I knew Madam Ranjeeva would notice. *"Would be way better with you here."*

"I promise she isn't so bad once you get to know her," he attempted to convince me.

I was in the midst of responding when I felt my mother nudge me. Madam Ranjeeva was indeed staring at me with her eyebrows raised.

"Oh, um, I'm sorry, Auntie," I fumbled. "Dev had just sent me a message so I was responding to him. He just wanted to make sure we had arrived."

She gave me a tight nod. "Please take a seat. Would you like some tea?"

"Yes, please."

"I'll ring for the maid."

Moments later, the housekeeper appeared with a tray carrying three cups of tea and several kinds of biscuits.

I accepted the teacup and dipped one of the biscuits into my tea.

"Be careful there, my dear. You wouldn't want to put on any more weight before the wedding."

I'm a size four, I grumbled in my head. I wasn't as thin as her but far from being heavy, and I had worked hard in my early twenties to get there after being slightly overweight much of my life. "Of course, Auntie," I remember saying as I forlornly placed the damp biscuit on the saucer. I sipped the tea in silence and stared at my feet.

Now it all seems ludicrous that I was so scared of your Dida. I think she would have appreciated me more if I had just stood up to her from the beginning. Of course, there's no way I could have known that at the time. Hindsight is always twenty-twenty. I hope you remember that when you look at some of the decisions you've made. I'm not sure how much I'll be able to remind you of this, so I'll have to count on you to remember.

Mom tried to make conversation to no avail. "I was so excited when Naina told me the news."

Madam Ranjeeva's eyes remained askance "Yes, well, you would be, wouldn't you?"

Several moments passed before she spoke again with her gaze directed at me. "Your mother is referring to the fact that you and my son have decided to marry, correct?"

"Yes, Auntie." I swallowed the lump in my throat.

"Indeed. Did you know that my son proposed to you without my consent?"

I bit down on my lip. "No, Auntie."

"Since he seems quite firm in this decision, there isn't much I can do about it. He made that abundantly clear when he chose to move in with you before you were even engaged. I will just have to accept it."

My nostrils flared. "Thank you so much, Auntie." I almost choked on the words.

"We now have the impossible task of preparing you, a working woman who has not spent a single moment in the public eye, to deal with it constantly."

I glowered at the floor as my future mother-in-law continued.

"The same applies to you, Rita," she said to my mother. "Both of you will require a completely new wardrobe. This kind of clothing…will not be appropriate." She gestured at our attire with a grimace. "Let me have our tailor get your measurements. We'll make all of the arrangements."

When the housekeeper came in to pick up our cups, Madam Ranjeeva spoke to her rapidly in Hindi.

At the time my Hindi wasn't as good as it is now, but I understood the gist of what she said. She asked the housekeeper to send over the tailor because we looked as if we were at a costume party. I was fuming—so angry with your father. I clenched my fists as visions of myself yelling at Dev appeared in front of me. *How could he send us into the lion's den without him?*

The next hour was torture. The tailor arrived, took our measurements, and received a number of barked instructions. I was completely at a loss. I have always considered myself someone who could warm to anyone, no matter the situation. Your Dida tested that assumption over and over in those first few days.

"Now that we've settled your clothing, we need to discuss everything that the press might be able to find on both of you." Madam Ranjeeva looked at me with stony eyes. "We need to know about every sexual partner you've had, every boyfriend, every stupid picture you've ever taken when you've been drinking. We need to see your social media sites, look into your connections, posts, groups, and any photos connected to you. As of this moment, make sure that everything is private and do not post on any of those sites until we give you the go-ahead, not even privately." She paused to take a sip of her tea, and I thought that might be all, but I was wrong.

"Naina, have you ever taken any drugs? Are you on birth control? Have you ever had an STD? Have you received any expensive gifts from your previous partners? Have you ever left anything out of a tax record on purpose? Have you ever colored outside of the lines in even the smallest fashion? You need to tell me everything. If there's a story that might come out, we need to know about it so that we can do preemptive damage control."

I clamped my jaw shut to keep from responding. My chest shook as I forced a long exhale before I let myself speak. "Auntie, is that really necessary? Would they really bother us in Paris?"

Madam Ranjeeva tilted her jaw and pinched her lips together. "My dear Naina, we are not worried about the reporters bothering you. My husband is the secretary of the treasury, and someday he may even run for president. I think the reporters might spend a bit more time on us than on your precious Parisian antiques. But if they find one negative thing in your past, it will reflect on us. If we don't deal with those problems now, they could become a major issue."

"Y-yes, of course. I'm sorry I didn't mean to imply—"

"No matter." She looked away from me toward my mom. "Rita, we will also need all of that same information from you."

Mom's mouth fell open before she could answer. "Certainly," she answered, and hesitated before continuing. "Would it be all right if I called you Komal?"

Madam Ranjeeva raised her eyebrows. "I suppose you must." She glanced at her watch. "Oh dear, I didn't realize that it was so late. I have another appointment, so I'm afraid that I must push you out."

"Of course. Thank you for having us." A slow smile spread across my face. We were going to be free. I resisted the urge to bolt for the door.

"It was a rather important obligation to have you here. Before you go, I must tell you that I will have our private investigator run basic background checks on you and the members of your family. He should be able to turn up any of the obvious things that could show up in the tabloids once we announce the engagement. Until then, you will not be able to wear that ring in public. Someone might recognize you," she said, pointing at my left hand.

I was so excited about our release that I didn't pay much attention to what she actually said. "Yes, Auntie," I mumbled. Only now do I know how pivotal that moment was.

"Thank you for having us, Komal."

"Very good. I'll see you in a couple of days once Dev arrives."

We left there in such a hurry that I didn't even internalize the meaning of the background check.

****

The next two days dragged by for us. I was still reeling from that afternoon, and I could only hope that Dev would be able to smooth things over once he arrived.

The hours crept by slowly. A few hours before Dev's flight arrived, the tailor delivered the clothes that his mother had commissioned for us. I didn't think it would be possible for a tailor to snub me, but I've never heard such disdain from a service professional. Nothing says budget like a Days Inn in Yonkers, I guess.

My face felt as if it were on fire when a black Lexus arrived with an entire new wardrobe of clothes for us. Don't get me wrong. The clothes were beautifully crafted, clearly made from the highest quality of fabrics. I just couldn't believe my own wardrobe was so inadequate as to merit such a gift. I scolded Dev for not telling me that his mother would never wear Indian clothes to meet us. Perhaps I could have tricked her with a dress from Banana Republic? I managed to convince him of that, but I knew that there was no way it would have worked. She would never have believed me if I had tried to pass off any of my clothing as being made by some fancy French designer.

On the morning after Dev arrived, we packed our stuff into a car sent to pick us up and returned to the Westchester mansion. *This is going to be a nightmare.* It echoed through my mind every few seconds on the way there. Were we insane to stay in the same house as a woman who didn't even think our clothes were good enough for her? I didn't realize at the time that things were going to get far worse before they took a turn for the better.

****

I was sweating profusely by the time we entered the drawing room at the Westchester mansion. In an effort to look presentable, I had put on a silky shift dress from my new tailored wardrobe. The cloth was soft and cool, but I still felt as if someone had wrapped me in a corset that was digging further and further into my chest and cutting off my airway. When we stepped inside, it took all of my self-control not to turn and flee for the hills.

"I see those clothes fit you both quite well," Madame Ranjeeva said, nodding toward us. "My tailor has outdone himself. I must see to it, however, that both of you see my stylist. You could do with some help on personal presentation as well."

My eyes flashed as my fear turned to anger. I scanned the room to look for my fiancé. *Where the hell is he?* I wanted to yell.

My prayers were answered when Dev finally walked into the room. "Sorry, sorry! I was stuck on a phone call," he said breathlessly. He gave his mother a kiss on the cheek, and then walked over to me to pull me into a bear hug. "I've missed you, babe," he whispered. "Sorry you had to deal with the first meeting on your own."

You will be. "Let's talk about it later," I answered in a hushed tone. "I missed you too."

"Could the two of you please spare us from this public display?" Madam Ranjeeva scowled. "We have important things to discuss. I have the results from the preliminary background check that our PI ran on both of you."

Dev separated from me as he gawked at his mother. "You ran a background check on them?"

"Of course. We live in the public eye. The press will dig up these skeletons anyway, so we had to be prepared. We had to do it before somebody else did. Besides, they both agreed to it. Didn't you?" Madam Ranjeeva shot a glance at the two of us. I could tell that she was daring us to contradict her.

I remember becoming especially interested in the pattern of the floor tiles at that particular moment. I kept my eyes firmly planted on the ground rather than making eye contact with either your Dida or your father.

"How dare you do that, Mother?" Dev asked.

"Do I really have to explain again—?"

"May I interject here, Komal?" Mom said, breaking into the conversation. "Since it's already been done, the reasons for it should be water under the bridge. We have nothing to hide, anyway, and the checks will confirm that. Now, you were about to tell us about the results." My affections for my mom were overflowing during that trip. She had promised me that she would support my marriage to Dev no matter what, and she had held her ground despite all of the previous insults from your Dida.

Madam Ranjeeva frowned and turned to her son. "Yes, indeed. We can discuss this later, Dev."

He glared at his mother. "We will, but for now, you can continue."

"The background checks have revealed several serious gaps that we will have to address preemptively to appease the voters. The press is going to come at us with everything that they have. I've scheduled appointments with my PR manager for you. He can talk through different details with each of you. I'm sure that he can address most everything, and that he will also insist that you both visit my stylist as soon as possible. But we do have one major concern from the background checks."

Dev crossed his arms. "Which is what exactly, Mother? That you didn't get to choose my bride?"

She rolled her eyes at Dev and turned toward my mom. "Rita, do you have a sister? A sister who abandoned her husband and six-year-old child to live in the Republic of East Africa? I'm sure that I don't have to explain how much damage control we will need if a member of your family is currently living in a country under a US embargo for harboring terrorists."

****

At that moment, Mom looked as if someone had sent a spear hurtling through the air straight at her heart. Of course, there's no way your Dida could have known how sensitive this subject would be for all of us, let alone how hard it would be on Mom. Madam Ranjeeva was only doing what she thought she needed to do for the sake of her family. Being a part of a political family is anything but fun and dandy. I'm sure you thought the Secret Service entourage was thrilling and kind of cool as a child, but it is a bit crippling for adults, which you've probably realized as you've grown older. Thankfully, we don't have to deal with it as much on a daily basis—just when we are visiting them.

At the time, I was angrier than anything else. I thought your Dida was incredibly insensitive, and I had no idea how to help Mom cope with the news. Everything with my aunt had happened when I was a kid, so I never had to be a supportive figure for Mom with that situation. I had memories, bits and pieces of arguments and conversations I had heard about my aunt who had abandoned her family, but I hadn't thought of them in years. Not consciously, at least. I'd never even told Dev about her.

Later that night, the two of us sat down to talk about it after we spent almost two hours convincing Mom to get some sleep. I sank down on the couch next to him, and he asked me what had happened that day.

"Naina, why didn't you ever tell me about your aunt?" he asked as he looked down into my eyes.

"I don't know. I haven't thought about her in so long. She's just not a part of our family any more. It wasn't on purpose." I remember trying to shrug it off. "I never realized that it would become an issue again. I mean, this is my family we're talking about, and every family has messed up bits in its history. Why should we have to put a spin on our past to appease a bunch of reporters?"

He stroked my hair softly. "I know it's not fair, babe, but we both know that this wouldn't have stayed a secret for long."

My voiced turned flat as I studied the wall behind his head. "I guess. It just makes me think of so many other things."

"What do you mean?"

"This isn't just a cover story for me, Dev. I really have no idea what happened to her. None of us do. And I have no clue about what happened to my cousin. The last time that I saw him was at my grandfather's funeral more than twenty years ago."

Dev wrapped his arm around me and squeezed my shoulder.

I blinked away tears. "My parents moved so much that we didn't see family a lot. But during the few visits when he was there, I had the little brother I had always wanted. Followed me around everywhere, my little shadow. I do remember that much. Then we lost him, and I never got the chance to know him." I shook my head. "He'd be around twenty-five now, and I don't even know what he looks like."

"What do you remember?"

"I remember my aunt vaguely. She's taller than my mom, with black curly hair. I think she's a doctor?" I shrugged. "I don't remember much of anything else. I remember my cousin running around everywhere and driving the adults crazy. When I was with my cousins, we were always laughing and running and playing. All three of us."

"You, him, and Shweta?"

"Yeah."

"That was the last time you saw him?"

I nodded. "Everything after that is murky. I remember hearing from someone that my aunt had left her family, and a conversation in the car one time when we were visiting Mom's brother, about how they'd heard from Nitu's father."

"Nitu? That's your cousin's name?"

"That's what we all called him. It's one of those Bengali nicknames. You know, I don't even know his real name. I don't think Mom does either. He was always just Nitu. We never used any other name within the family, and we never interacted with them outside of home."

Dev frowned. "Nicknames are different for me, so I'm not sure I get it. Neither of you know his real name?"

"I don't think so," I sighed. "You have to understand, though…within our family, his name *is* Nitu. Using that *daak nam* is supposed to mean that we are closer to him than anyone who uses his real name. It's a little strange for me too because I didn't really grow up there either. If we'd been around him more, I'm sure we would have heard his real name. I'd have seen him use it with school friends or for some kind of official documentation." I paused. "Or if Mom had been closer to my aunt when he was born, then she'd at least know it. But we were already far away, and she didn't have any more time with him than I did. Plus, she and my aunt were already distant by then."

"What do you know about his dad? Anything from that conversation you overheard?"

"My aunt was always the breadwinner in their family, so when she left, they didn't have anything. Nitu's father called my uncle—Sameer *Mama*—when things became desperate. He said that they didn't have any money left and he didn't know what to do." I tried to catch my breath. "They—my aunt and uncle—told him to send Nitu to them, told him that they would take care of him."

"So what happened?"

"They never heard from him again. He never showed up with Nitu. My family tried looking for him, but we couldn't locate them."

"Wow."

"The only other thing I remember is that my aunt called Mom one day from Taisoun. It was right after we moved, so I was probably thirteen at the time. She called to ask my parents to help process her immigration to Canada. Mom just blew up and hung up on her. It was awful. I had no idea she was still living there."

Dev kissed my forehead. "Babe, it's going to be okay, I promise. We'll figure something out. Let's just take your mom out tomorrow and help her forget about all of this."

I gave him a half smile. "Good luck getting her to do anything."

"Your mom loves me. She'll listen to anything I say."

My smile widened. "Thank you," I whispered. I was happy with the idea of trying to forget about the whole thing. We could let the politicians handle the politics and get on with our lives. But at the back of my mind, the first seed had already sprouted. Nitu and his father couldn't have disappeared without a trace. *What if I could find them?*

****

March, 2017 – My decision

I always wanted a little brother. Apparently, when I was little, I used to bug my mom by saying that she should give me a little brother, but I still ended up being an only child. Perhaps that was why the prospect of finding Nitu captivated me so much. I would gain a sibling if I could find him.

My feelings about my aunt were more ambivalent. Where did she go and why did she disappear? I had only met her a few times, but I found it impossible to reconcile that question with the faint memories of a smiling woman who chased us around the house in Calcutta. Or should I say *Kolkata*? I've never been able to get used to the city's name change to Kolkata because I didn't grow up with it. The same goes for Mumbai versus Bombay, although I do find that one easier since it happened when I was much younger.

Instead of dwelling on my questions surrounding my aunt's disappearance, I pushed them aside to focus on using her as a means to an end. If no one in my family could remember Nitu's real name, I would have to find someone who did.

Dev snuck a look at the background check, but it unfortunately didn't include my cousin's name. I still hadn't told him that I was thinking of trying to find Nitu, so he acted on my request oblivious to the plan I had started to hatch. In his subconscious, he probably knew what I was doing, but sometimes it's easier to pretend than to acknowledge the truth.

He was able to find the name of my aunt's previous husband, Mokul Chatterjee, but looking for a name like that in Bengal was akin to trying to find someone named Matthew Smith in Boston. It's why my family had no success when looking for him so many years earlier. The private detective's file focused on my mom, so the details on my aunt were a bit bare. The file said nothing about where she had lived previously and provided little detail other than the fact that she was practicing medicine in East Africa. It wasn't even clear where the private detective had found the information about her current location. The last time that she had spoken to my mom was fifteen years earlier, and had it not been for the report, none of us would have suspected that she was still living there. However, the file did contain an address in Om Tais, a suburb just outside of the capital, Taisoun, and a phone number for the landline at that residence. It also included a list of known associates, which included three other doctors and some random East African names, so I mostly disregarded it. Most importantly, the file included her real name, Trina Banerjee. As with Nitu, I had only known her as *Mashi.* I held on to both of those pieces of information as the only real links I had to her identity, and through her, to Nitu.

I'm not sure when I really made up my mind to make the trip to East Africa. Everything just seemed to point toward it. The company I worked for had given me extended leave. I requested it originally so that I could help my mother-in-law with wedding planning in New York, but it turned out to be a blessing as I started to search for Nitu. Dev's business was taking off, which meant that he would be traveling quite a bit during the next two or three months, so I wouldn't be neglecting him while I traveled. I was confident that I would be able to find her using the information in the investigation file. I'm sure that thinking must have been incredibly naïve, but I did manage to get lucky. I could have tried following up with the PI to get more information on Nitu, but I didn't want to risk giving him any more information about what I was seeking. I was also sure that he would take it directly to Dev's mom, and I wanted to keep her very much at arm's length. More than anything, I was scared of how she would interpret my actions. I could think of a number of adjectives at the time. *Reckless. Untrustworthy. Selfish. Obstinate. Inconsiderate. Uncontrollable. Pigheaded. Irresponsible. Self-centered. Rash.* I was so sure she would spew them at Dev if she found out about my plans. She was reluctant to accept our engagement, and I didn't want to provide her with any more fuel. In my mind, I had created the ultimate villain who hoped to breathe fire on our relationship. I took this analogy so far down the rabbit hole that I didn't even use all of the resources at my disposal to find Nitu.

I don't know when I decided that I owed it to myself to take the plunge. I remember taking a walk around the grounds of the mansion by myself. I strolled along at a leisurely pace, and it took me almost an hour to reach what is now my favorite spot. You know the one—the small rock garden next to the babbling brook. Your Dadu's mentor had willed the property to him when he died. Without any succeeding heirs, he had left your Dadu a short note that read: *You have been like a son to me. Therefore, you inherit all of my responsibilities as well as my lures.* That spot always made me feel a little better about the opulence of the entire place, with the reminder that Dev's family had never purchased it outright.

As I stood there watching the brook, I let my thoughts drift over the previous few days. I replayed the moment when your Dida unintentionally released one of our oldest and most terrible family secrets. The emotions surrounding it weren't based on scandal. We simply didn't know what had happened. We had no knowledge of affairs or adultery. All we had was the fact that my aunt could abandon her son. It was a shocking truth. There was no way to spin it that didn't make me question how my Mashi—my aunt—could have done what she did. *Why?* I wondered repeatedly. Perhaps there was some mitigating factor? Something that no one in the family knew? A mother's job is to protect and nurture, to guide, and to provide her child with the best shot in life that she can. Sometimes the best way to do that is not always clear.

I thought of Nitu. My recollection of him was nothing more than a faint sketch in the corners of my mind. As I walked through the rock garden, I remember searching for my emotional bearings. It seemed surreal. *He would be in his midtwenties right about now.* I couldn't get around that thought. The only picture that I could imagine was of his five-year-old self, running around, giggling and playing tag and hide-and-seek. I could remember one moment in particular. We were playing tag when Mashi came into the living room looking for him. She'd just returned from the grocery store and was about to make him take a bath. She had a large bag of sweets in her hand that she had just bought. When she called for him, he swooped in, grabbed the bag of sweets, and bolted into the bedroom before anyone had the chance to react. Mashi laughed about it with Mom and their brother late into the night after making sure that she had scolded Nitu royally and put him to bed immediately after dinner. She never knew that Nitu and I were creeping around with our other cousin, Shweta, and heard the whole conversation. He'd even managed to save us some of the sweets before handing the bag to his mother on the way to the bathtub.

It was the only memory of him that I could summon. I couldn't really remember his face, only that he had bright eyes and a smile that lit everything up around him. I closed my eyes, struggling to find any other vision of him that was stored somewhere in the back of my mind. If it indeed existed, I was nowhere close to being able to unlock it. Maybe if I'd had pictures of him, he would be more ingrained in my memory. I was close to so many family friends and distant cousins, but I was unable to go further than that one memory of Nitu.

As I looked out at the vast landscape before me, I replayed that single memory. I hadn't thought of it in years, but it now held a prominent place in the center of my thoughts. That was probably the point of no return. I may not have admitted it to myself, but I had just decided that I had to try to find him.

Three days passed before I had the courage to speak to Dev about it.

"I want to find her," I remember saying.

"Who?" His forehead crinkled.

"You know. Mashi."

A shadow passed across his face. "You mean…in East Africa?" he whispered.

I nodded, and we simply stared at each other, neither saying a word.

When he didn't respond, I tried to make my case. "Dev, the file has her address in it. I could just go and talk to her. I only need a few days to go there. I could find out about my cousin, maybe even get enough information to find him afterward."

"Can't you just get that from John?" he asked, referring to his mother's PI.

I shook my head.

"There must be records—birth details, something." He looked at me puzzled.

"We don't even know Nitu's real name. There's no way we could find him without that."

"What about her ex-husband, your uncle? Didn't the file have his name in it?"

"Yes, it did," I said softly. "But I'd never be able to find a man named Mokul Chatterjee in Bengal. He could be anywhere. I'm sure every Bengali person I know is at least acquainted with someone who has that name, but none of them would be the one I'm looking for." I took his hands and squeezed them softly. "We need more than that. I have to do this. If I don't, I'm always going to wonder if I should have. I have the time off from work, and we don't have crazy family obligations yet. I need this."

"Naina, I don't know. Is it even safe for you to go?"

"Taisoun is probably safer than New York. Everything I've read supports that. No one will even think that I'm a foreigner."

He frowned. "Do you really have to do this now?"

"The longer we wait, the less likely it is that I find either of them."

"Fine. But let me send someone with you. We can hire a security guard." We both knew that he would never win that battle, but he tried anyway.

I smiled softly. "Because that wouldn't be conspicuous at all. That will just make me look like I have something worth stealing. I won't do anything stupid, I promise. I've been all over Africa for work already. Taisoun can't be that different. Besides, Faisal is there working at the UN. He'll make sure that I'm well looked after."

Dev's face flushed red. "I'm sure he wouldn't mind taking care of you."

"Oh, because you have so much to worry about," I said as I shot him a look. Dev knew that Faisal had asked me out on a date when we were in college. He'd also come to visit me in Paris on a stopover a few years earlier. It was about two weeks before Dev finally asked me out, although we'd been flirting for the better part of a month. I've never seen your father so jealous as when he heard about how your Uncle Faisal had tried to make a move before he'd worked up the nerve to do the same. They may seem to be great friends now, but it took some time for your father to work past that, silly man. I resisted the urge to tease him about that; I wanted to focus on convincing him to let me go.

We argued about the details for the next hour, but I had no intention of conceding. I had made up my mind. I promised to call him as often as possible and send him e-mails and messages on the days in between. The next morning, I applied for my visa with Faisal's help. Fifteen days later, I boarded a flight to Taisoun.

****

As a city, Taisoun was more developed than I could have possibly imagined. It felt like a combination of some of the other Arab cities that I had visited. The deep blue of the two halves of the Naifa River coming together was reminiscent of the sea near Tunis. The smattering of modern buildings along the coast looked comparable to a less concentrated version of recent Dubai real estate. The vendors on the streets who didn't seem to pay any attention as you walked by were more similar to Kuwait. But when I walked across the bridge in front of my hotel to go over to Sanvia Island, the chaos on the other side took me to Cairo. In some ways, that chaos also reminded me of time spent in New York City when I had to push my way between the various stalls along the streets of Manhattan's Chinatown. The mishmash all around meant that I felt both at home there and like a complete foreigner.

I tried the phone number at my aunt's house that evening and left a message on the answering machine for her to call me on the disposable phone I'd purchased from a local street vendor. "I'm here about some urgent family business at the wishes of Sunita Banerjee,"

I said into the machine, using my grandmother's name. *I hope she responds.*

I made up my mind that if I did not hear from her within the next twenty-four hours, I would just make my way to her house. The city seemed organized enough that a taxi would be able to find the address in Om Tais on the other side of the river.

Later that evening, I met Faisal for dinner. He picked me up at the hotel and drove us to a local fish restaurant. We threw around old stories and feasted on a giant mound of fried fish accompanied by a spicy peanut sauce that was, in my mind, an East African delicacy. I topped it off with a glass of fresh watermelon juice and leaned back, taking in the moment. The juice was so sweet that I could feel the sugar rush surpassing my jet lag with each sip.

"Naina, we've talked about everything except the most important topic," Faisal said after we had gone through all of the catching up we could potentially do in an hour-long dinner. "What are you doing here? Is your company trying to do business in East Africa?"

"No, I, er, I'm just here for a visit." My eyes danced around the patio behind him, avoiding his gaze.

"Sure," he said, chuckling. "This is really the ultimate destination to visit as a tourist right now. Especially alone." He threw his hands out to the sides. "Don't get me wrong, there are beautiful sites here. I just wouldn't picture it as a spot on the general tourist radar."

My face broke into a smile. "Since when am I a normal tourist?"

"I'm just surprised that you would come here so all of a sudden. And without Dev?"

"I thought you told me Taisoun was perfectly safe."

"Don't be silly. It is safe here, but that doesn't make it a vacation destination. So tell me what's going on."

"I found out something…about someone in my family." I sighed, hesitating. "My mother's sister disappeared when I was a kid. We heard that she was here once, but then she disappeared and we never heard from her again."

"Okay," he said as he tilted his head to the side.

"I found something that says that she might still be here."

"In Taisoun?"

I nodded. "In Om Tais, actually, but yeah."

"Wow. Why are you here alone then? Why didn't your mom come with you?"

The sides of my mouth flickered with embarrassment as I looked at the floor. "I haven't told her yet."

"Naina, you're going to get yourself into trouble. You have to tell your mom. You're here to look for her sister."

"I know, I know," I chuckled. "They just didn't have the best relationship, and I'm not sure how Mom will react. Besides, I might not even find her."

Faisal crossed his arms. "If you have her address in Om Tais, then I'd be surprised if you didn't. In all seriousness, though, when are you going to see her?"

"I don't know. I left a voice mail at her house this afternoon. I guess I'll give her a day to call me back."

"I see," he nodded. "Why don't we just drive over there now? I don't have to come in with you, but I can be there for some added support if you want."

"No, I'm not ready. I need to be more mentally prepared," I shook my head. "I still don't know what I'm going to say."

"When you said she disappeared…what happened to her? You meant that she left, right?"

"Yeah. I don't know how I feel about her, or any of this. I know my mom is still probably furious at her. But maybe I'm more curious." I shrugged my shoulders. "I did come all this way, but I don't know what to expect. I just don't know."

Faisal gave me a comforting look. "I think it's okay for you to be curious. You don't have to be angry if that's not how you feel."

"I guess." I glanced down at my plate. "She did a horrible thing."

"You mean by leaving?"

"When she left, she was her family's breadwinner. They had a son," I whispered.

"So she left him?" His jaw set ever so slightly.

"Yeah."

I turned my attention back to the fish until a huge yawn came at me from the waist up. The sugar from the watermelon juice was starting to wear off. "Wow," I said. "I guess jet lag has come to find me."

"You've had a long journey. Let's go. I'll drive you."

"Thanks, Faisal. And thanks for listening to me go on about this."

"What are friends for? I just wish I could help. Let me know if you want some extra support in Om Tais. Even if you don't want me to come with you, I can set you up with a taxi driver. I know him pretty well and he won't pull anything with the fares. That way I'll at least know that you're safe."

"Okay, sounds good."

When I made it up to my room, I checked for voice mail messages on my disposable cell phone. As soon as the recording said, "You have no new messages," I crashed directly onto the bed. Part of me was disappointed, but the other part was relieved.

****

The next morning I awoke to the loud buzzing of my disposable cell phone.

"Hello," I mumbled. I tried to rub the sleep out of my eyes, but the jet lag was stubborn.

"Hi, this is Trina Banerjee returning your call. You said you had urgent information about my mother, Sunita?"

I sat up abruptly and the remainder of my sleepiness fell away. "Er, yes, yes I do."

The line went silent for a moment. "What is it? Does this have something to do with her estate?"

"Perhaps we'd best meet in person, M-Miss Banerjee," I managed to blurt out.

My heartbeat echoed in my ears as I waited for her to respond.

"Certainly. Where are you staying?"

"The Corinthia Hotel."

"Burj al Khaleej?" she asked, using the previous name of the hotel.

"Yes."

"Okay. I can meet you at the downstairs café after work this evening. Around six probably."

"Okay, great." *I'm Rita* didi*'s daughter, Naina.* It was on the tip of my tongue. I almost said it, but something stopped me. Would she be more or less likely to want to see me if I told her? Would she even believe it? I hadn't seen her in more than twenty years. I could probably pass for anyone. "My name is, er, Naina Ranjeeva, for your reference," I said, using my soon-to-be married name.

"I'll see you at six then."

****

The minutes seemed to crawl by for the rest of the day. I walked to the national museum and spent almost three hours browsing through the country's extensive history. The collection consisted of artifacts from the old Egyptian civilization that took my breath away. I'd completely forgotten that the two countries were originally part of one civilization. Upstairs there were numerous statues and paintings from more recent eras. In the courtyard outside of the museum, the staff had reconstructed some of the older temples that were once located on the banks of the Naifa. The new dams and reservoirs along the river had threatened their structural integrity, so the government had relocated the stones to the capital where the temples had been rebuilt. The site was amazing and even made me forget how slowly the minutes of the day were trickling by.

In the two hours that I spent at the museum, I marveled that I was almost the only visitor. One family of expatriates, probably Italians, came in after me.

I returned to the hotel and spent an hour at the downstairs gym and spa before deciding to venture out once again. Faisal had the afternoon off and joined me. We walked toward the confluence point of the two halves of the Naifa River. It took about thirty minutes along the banks of the East Naifa as it passed around the southern part of Sanvia Island. He pointed out a number of landmarks—Friendship Hall, one of the premiere event spaces in the city, the old Hilton Hotel that had been renamed Seaway after the effects of the US trade embargo, and some of the different ministries that visible from South Naifa Street.

At the confluence point, we stopped at a small park and sat down on a bench. I gazed out over the converging waters and looked around wistfully. "You know what's amazing?"

"You like it here," he said with a smile.

"I do. I didn't expect to. What I was actually going to say is that no one has tried to sell us anything. We just walked thirty minutes on one of the city's busiest streets and no one bothered us."

"That's not the personality here. Back home in Cairo, we would have been assaulted at least fifty times to buy handicrafts and food, and let's not forget the carriage rides."

I could see the nostalgia on his face. "Do you miss home?"

"Oh, of course. You know how it is there—all of the craziness and the intensity. But this is nice too. I just wish things were going better for people here."

"What do you mean? They don't seem that poor or distressed."

"They aren't in the grander scheme of things. But most people here are well educated, yet they're just doing random jobs because whatever work they were doing before the embargo has dried up."

"What about people who are younger?"

Faisal shrugged. "Education here used to be one of the best in all of the Arab countries. It's still not bad, but it's not that great either. So it's just more of the same. Maybe losing the oil to the south will help move things along a bit more. There's a lot of pressure on the government to make sure that things don't completely fall apart now. The atmosphere is pretty tense."

"Most of the oil went to the south after partition?" I asked.

"Yeah. There are still a couple of disputed areas, but most of it has already been agreed upon."

"I see."

"Anyway, let's talk about something else, something less depressing," he said with a sigh. "So you and Dev are finally getting married?"

The abrupt change of subject made me uncomfortable for a moment. "We are indeed. Sometime next spring probably."

"You don't wear your ring when you travel?" he motioned toward my hand.

"It's at the hotel in the safe. I figured it would be better not to attract too much attention."

He grinned. "Taisoun's probably safer for that than Paris. No one ever gets mugged here. There's no violent crime."

"Whatever you say." I rolled my eyes. "Tell me more about you and your life here. Are you having fun? Do you like working with the UN?"

"More or less. Work is good. I'm close to home and close to family. It's easy for me to get a quick flight out and spend a weekend in Cairo. My mom certainly loves that I'm this close."

I crossed my arms. "Am I sensing a 'but' here…?"

"My family keeps bugging me to settle down. I actually started dating this East African girl, but things didn't work out."

"I'm sorry to hear that," I said with a frown. "What happened?"

"I just didn't feel that I was ready to get married, and there was too much pressure from both of our families to do so. So we decided to just be friends."

"I'm sure that's working out really well for both of you." I tilted my head in amusement. We both knew what I was thinking.

Faisal narrowed his eyes at me. "Whatever. We're dealing with it." He crossed his arms. "I guess you're right. We'll probably get back together. I just want to get to know her a bit more before we take that step."

My expression brightened and my eyes lit up. "So this is pretty serious then. You're unofficially together, and you're thinking about getting married."

His face flushed. "I guess so."

"So where do old college friends fall in the likelihood of getting to meet your unofficial girlfriend whom you are thinking of proposing to?"

"You want to meet her?"

I gestured widely with my hands. "No shit I want to meet her."

Faisal pressed his fist against his lips. "You're meeting your aunt tonight, right?"

"Yeah."

"How about this? We'll pick you up after and you can tell us all about what happened."

I bit down on my lip. "Are you sure? That's a bit heavy for the first time that I meet her isn't it?"

"Don't worry about it. I'm sure you'll need the distraction. I'll give her a heads up that things are pretty intense for you right now."

"Thanks."

Ten minutes later, we walked back to the hotel. Once I made it to my room, I spent an hour in the bathtub trying to figure out how I was supposed to feel about the upcoming meeting. *Shouldn't I be angry? Upset?* I remember asking myself. I knew my mom would be, but the situation was not the same for me. The only emotional reaction I could pinpoint was some combination of distance and curiosity.

****

April, 2017 – The Republic of East Africa

I went downstairs a little before six, feeling numb. I took a seat at a table in the café and ordered a tonic water. With the first sip, I wished fervently that I could spike it with some gin. I usually only enjoyed the occasional drink, but I had never wanted to rely on liquid courage more than at that point. No such luck in a dry country.

I was halfway through the drink when a flustered-looking woman entered the café. She glanced around, clearly in search of someone or something. She looked to be in her midfifties and her curly black hair and café-au-lait skin were similar to my own. I don't know if it was the way she seemed to be searching for someone, or the way she looked, but I recognized her instantly. I could see some of my grandfather in her stature, and you've seen how much she looks like Mom. I stood up and waved at her.

As soon as she saw me, her face turned ashen. She approached slowly, staring, gaping. She looked as if she'd just seen a ghost. "Who are you?" she mumbled.

"Mashi, I'm Naina. Rita didi's daughter," I said in Bengali.

Her eyes bore into me in silence, and I squirmed under her gaze. She opened her mouth a few times to say something and closed it again. I watched her blink away some scattered tears welling up in her eyes.

What am I supposed to do now? I remember asking myself. *Should I comfort her? What for?*

Those thoughts became even more pressing as she took a step toward me and wrapped her arms around me in a hug. My eyes widened as I looked past her shoulder around the restaurant. *Ack.*

When she finally released me, we both collapsed into the chairs on either side of the table.

"You look just like your mother," she whispered. Her face broke out into a smile. The new emotion crossing her face changed it completely as the smile touched each of her features.

I felt a flash of recognition. *Nanni. She has Nanni's smile.*

I took a deep breath and tried to form words. "That's what people tell me," I managed to muster.

She dabbed her face with a tissue, sniffling. "They aren't wrong." She gave me a tearful smile. "You know, when you said your name was Naina, I thought *maybe*, for a second. But then I thought it couldn't be. Why didn't you tell me who you were on the phone?"

"I don't know." I shook my head. "I wasn't sure if it would make you more or less likely to come."

Her eyes went blank. "Of course I would have come." Her voice was shaky and unconvincing.

I bit down on my lip and directed my gaze toward the table. *Now what?*

The waiter answered my prayers for distraction when he came by to ask for our order. She ordered a grilled chicken sandwich along with an Ethiopian coffee, and I asked for the same.

"Have you had Ethiopian coffee before?" she asked once the waiter had stepped away. It was a valiant attempt at meaningless conversation.

"No, actually."

The fan above our heads became very loud as I focused my attention on anything except her face. The emotion rooted there was too overwhelming. I had no idea what I was expecting, but all I knew is that it wasn't that. In some crazy fashion, I had hoped that the conversation would just flow—nothing like the pure awkwardness that confronted me.

I'm sure she felt the strangeness of that moment too. She must have felt odd about how far I was from being able to reciprocate the level of emotion she had just demonstrated. Yet, I had made such a long journey just to see her. What could I possibly want from her?

I had no idea how to answer that question myself.

Those thoughts were silenced temporarily when Mashi spoke again. "Does she know that you are here?" I could tell how hard it was for her to ask the question. Her voice was trembling and her right hand shook as she reached for another tissue.

"You mean my mom?"

"Yes."

I shook my head.

A few more tears rolled slowly down her face.

There were things that I wanted to say to her. I wanted to explain why I had decided not to tell my mom about the trip, but instinct told me to comfort the woman sitting in front of me. Someone in pain deserved comfort. It was a simple human reaction, but in the back of my mind, I knew that I was supposed to be angry, supposed to be hurt. At that moment, I didn't care how I was supposed to feel, though. As I watched her sob in front of me, I felt obligated to explain all of that pain away. I opened my mouth to explain, to say something, anything to ease her distress, but the words would not come. The distance between us held my tongue. More than twenty years since the last time that we had spoken.

Almost fourteen years since she had tried to speak to anyone in my family.

She took it in and nodded, wiping her nose again. She kept her eyes averted until she spoke again. "How did you find me?"

I shrugged. "There aren't that many Trina Banerjees living in East Africa."

"You knew I was here?"

"Not exactly," I said with a frown. *How much could I tell her about the background check?* I decided to keep that information close to the chest and bend the truth a little. "I remembered a conversation from when I was a kid. You called my parents to ask for their help to get Canadian immigration. You told my mom that you were in East Africa."

Mashi looked up from the floor and swallowed loudly. "I remember that. You were there when I spoke to them?"

"Yes."

Her cheeks burned red. "I'm sorry you had to hear that."

I hesitated. "Er, it's okay."

"Naina, tell me. Why did you decide to come here? That conversation…it must have been fifteen years ago."

I bit down on my lip to stop myself from blurting out the whole truth. "I just thought it was time. I do a lot of work in Africa now and I was nearby, so I decided to come here to try to find you. I wanted to see if I could."

"Thank you for coming," she said softly.

"Sure." I tried to keep my voice from sounding as aloof as I felt.

"So tell me, what kind of work do you do? What brings you to different parts of Africa? Maybe I can see you more often, more than just this trip."

"Maybe. Sure. I, er, work in international development consulting."

"Oh, I see," she said. "Did you go back to Canada? When I spoke to your parents, I guess you were in Kuwait."

"No. I moved to the US for school, but then went to graduate school in Europe. We live in Paris now."

Her face brightened. "We?" Her gaze shifted to my bare hand. "Are you married now?"

"About to be."

"Congratulations."

"Thank you, Mashi," I said stiffly. "So, what about you? Have you been living here, since then? Are you still practicing medicine?"

"Yes, I am. I work at a hospital in Om Tais on the other side of the river. Sometimes I also do volunteer work in other parts of the country."

"Other parts of East Africa? Where do you go?"

"It varies. I've made a lot of trips to the southern provinces in the past five years."

"Wow. Is it dangerous?"

She shrugged. "Maybe, but not as bad as you would think. There aren't a lot of bombings or attacks, but the number of people who need help is overpowering. All of the refugee camps—you know, people living in such close proximity without good sanitation and quality food. It breeds all kinds of diseases. We always have our hands full."

My phone buzzed and intruded on the conversation. I checked my messages and saw that Faisal and his girlfriend, Arya, were on their way to pick me up.

"I actually have to go soon," I said softly. Secretly, I was grateful. I could only endure the stale, stilted conversation for so long. "I'm sorry to cut this short."

"It's okay," she nodded. "How long are you staying?"

"Probably until the end of the week."

"Would you come over for dinner tomorrow? I can have a car pick you up here at the hotel."

I searched my mind frantically for a reason to decline, but came up blank. I pursed my lips. "Dinner? Sure…dinner sounds great."

"Good." She beamed at me. "You'll get to meet my husband as well."

Husband? Since she hadn't changed her name, the thought of a new husband hadn't occurred to me. I remembered the list of known associates in her file, which I had disregarded as doctors or medical professionals whom she worked with at the hospital. I took a deep breath and controlled my response. "Your husband?" I forced a smile on to my face. "That sounds, yes, that would be great."

She gave me another awkward hug and left the table smiling. As soon as she was out of sight, I bolted.

****

"How are you doing?" Faisal asked as I got into the passenger seat of his car.

I shook my head. "I don't know. It was fine I guess. Just so awkward. Maybe I should have expected it, but I didn't."

"Are you okay?"

"I don't know." I bit my lip as I replayed the conversation in my head. "She has a husband now. She remarried and we had no idea."

"Oh. Does that make you mad?"

"No, not really," I said. "But I feel as if it should. You know, she ran away from her family and just found herself a new one. She didn't care to get in touch with us, not even to tell us about her new husband, so why should I make all of this effort for her?"

"I see." He reached over and patted me on the knee. "It's only natural for you to feel this way."

"Maybe. I promised her I would have dinner with them tomorrow. I don't know what I'm going to say."

"Dinner? With both of them. Wow. Well, that could be good…I hope?" he suggested.

"I guess. What are we going to talk about? The only things I know about her have to do with my family. The one she left behind without a second thought."

"You don't know that she hasn't thought about you in all those years. Maybe she was just too scared to approach any of you."

"If that's true, should she really get credit for that? She still let that dictate her actions. Besides, we don't even know if that's the case. For all I know, she walked away without looking back."

Faisal nodded. "You could be right, but I hope not. What about your cousin? You could talk about him."

"Talk about him with her husband right there? He might not even know about her son."

"Try not to worry so much, Naina. You'll figure it out."

I let out a long sigh. "I hope you're right. Anyway, dude, where's your lady?"

A smile splashed across his face. "She had to run a quick errand. We're on our way to pick her up."

"Good. I was afraid that you'd decided to keep her hidden," I said with a goofy expression on my face. "I'm glad I get to meet her."

We pulled into a grocery store parking lot and he pointed out of the window. "There she is."

A slim woman in a long green traditional East African dress that bore a remarkable resemblance to a sari walked over to our car.

We spent the rest of the evening catching up and getting to know one another. We spoke about anything and everything, except for my awkward encounter with my aunt.

****

The next morning passed more quickly than that of the previous day. The night before, Faisal had taken us to a tiny restaurant run out of someone's home in the northern part of Taisoun, and we stayed there until the wee hours of the morning. It was clearly an underground establishment, not only because of the setting, but they also served us a number of different alcoholic beverages to accompany the meal. As you'll remember from your graduation party, I have a very low tolerance, so the evening became something of a drunken haze. I don't remember all of the details, but suffice it to say, my friends made sure that my mind was distracted from the conversation with Mashi and the upcoming dinner.

With some effort, I managed to sleep in for a while the next morning. I woke up every hour after the sun first appeared to guzzle another glass of water. I was able to stave off the worst of my hangover, but I still had a gut-wrenching headache when I finally crawled out of bed at 11:15 a.m. Somehow I dragged myself downstairs to the gym, but was only able to run a grand total of two minutes and thirty-five seconds. At the end of it, I went back upstairs and collapsed onto my bed to sleep some more. When I woke up three hours later, my head still felt foggy, but the excruciating pain had departed. I went through the motions of showering and turned my attention to my computer. My company had requested some input on a specific document, even though I was on leave, and I had planned to spend a few hours looking at it that day. Thankfully, the deadline was not for another week, so I gave up on that daunting task and watched three episodes of *JAG* instead to pass the time. By the time evening rolled around, I was almost grateful. The hangover had destroyed most of my day, which had helped move the hours along. At five thirty, I changed into some nicer clothes and went downstairs to wait for Mashi's car.

****

The sun was setting as the driver drove me west toward Om Tais. The sky was lit up in sharp pinks and yellows. We drove across the bridge that passed over the confluence point of the East and West Naifa Rivers, and the sight astounded me again. *This trip might be worth it just for getting to see this,* I told myself. I could only hope that the interaction this evening would not be as awkward as I had foreseen.

A few minutes later, we drove up to the house. I'll never forget how it looked. It was beautiful. With its flat roof and large terraces, it reminded me of Arab homes I'd seen in richer neighborhoods in Kuwait and other parts of the Middle East. The cream-colored stone is common in the richer neighborhoods in Taisoun. I walked up to the gate and rang the bell while the driver parked in a garage at the end of a long driveway.

My stomach was in knots by the time someone came out and opened the door. The woman who opened it was dressed in traditional clothing. Her features were soft and her skin flawless. She couldn't have been much older than I was at the time.

Without introducing herself, she led me to the house in silence and opened the door to the entryway adjacent to the living room. I turned around and said, "Shukran," meaning *thank you*, but she was already gone. I removed my shoes in the entryway and took a seat in the living room. Several sculptures on display cast dark gray shadows across the walls of the dimly lit space. The ceilings were high and the couch gave me a view of a long dramatic staircase that wrapped around a corner of the room.

"Naina, I'm so sorry I didn't come to pick you up myself," I heard from behind me.

I turned around and saw Mashi coming out of the kitchen in a green apron that covered a dark blue dress.

"It's okay," I said. I wasn't expecting her to appear from behind me so I tried to gather my thoughts quickly. I pasted a smile on my face as she approached. She came up to me and gave me another one of those hugs. *Dear God. So awkward,* a voice screamed in my head.

"Now please sit down," Mashi said once she released me. "What can I get for you? We have a few different kinds of juice, of course some soda, and some East African cider. And if you're in the mood for something more alcoholic, I can supply that too."

The thought of alcohol made me mentally groan, but I was a little tempted to indulge. *Maybe it would make this dinner more tolerable.* I debated for a moment and then went with the safe choice. "I'll just have some juice."

"Would you like sugar added to your juice? I only ask because that's the standard custom here, but I've never been able to get used to it."

I shook my head. "No sugar for me."

She poured me a glass of watermelon juice from a pitcher in the living room. It was cold, fresh, and delicious. I savored the taste. It offered a momentary respite from the jolting conversation that I knew was about to begin.

"I'm so sorry, but my husband's been held up on a business trip. He was supposed to be home this morning, but his flight was canceled, so he won't get in until tomorrow. He sends his regards and apologies."

I felt a weight lift from my shoulders. "Oh, that's okay," I said brightly. "I completely understand. These things happen, of course."

Mashi removed her apron and took a seat on a chair across from me in the living room. "Dinner will be ready in just a moment. Are you hungry?"

"Yes, I am. I'm looking forward to a home-cooked meal."

"Have you tried much East African food?"

"A little. I've had some great fish and chicken over the past couple of days."

"Okay, good. So you haven't had the traditional-style goat meat yet?" Mashi asked.

"No, I don't think so."

"Well, you are about to. Along with *foul medamas* and some other traditional dishes. If you've traveled around the Middle East, you've probably had some similar things, but I'm partial to the East African way of cooking."

"Thank you so much. That sounds wonderful," I compelled myself to say. Not that I wasn't thankful for some delicious food, of course, because I most certainly was. I just had no idea how to start a conversation that went beyond small talk.

"Oh, of course. You're very welcome. It's not often that I get to see my niece."

"Do you cook mostly East African dishes now?" I asked.

"Not all the time. I enjoy cooking traditional East African, but sometimes I make Bengali food—you know, like *ilish mach* and *chanar dalna*," she said, naming some signature Bengali dishes.

"I also make a lot of different, more eclectic things," Mashi continued. "Sometimes I make pasta and more Italian dishes, or different types of meat. All kinds of stuff. I do really enjoy cooking. It's great that I have help in the kitchen now, but I still prefer to cook on my own. What about you? Do you cook?"

"Yes, I love cooking. I find it very therapeutic. I love experimenting and making up new recipes. I usually read several before I come up with something of my own, depending on what ingredients I have available."

"It's always fun to substitute different ingredients and see what happens. It's pretty easy while cooking, but much harder with baking. I found that out the hard way when I tried to improvise my way through a recipe for German chocolate cake," she said with a chuckle. "I don't enjoy that nearly as much."

"I enjoy baking too, but I know what you mean. You have to be a lot more careful about substitution and experimentation when you're baking. It's also a lot easier to fix if something goes wrong when you're cooking—you can make different adjustments if too much of one spice went in or something. That's a lot harder to do when baking." *We're actually having a conversation?*

We were interrupted by a signal from one of the kitchen staff. "Dinner is served. Shall we go eat?" Mashi asked.

"Yes, of course."

I followed her into the dining room, which was set up with a real East African feast. There was a fresh mutton stew, the spicy peanut sauce I was growing to love, an assortment of vegetables both in a salad and cooked, and the full set-up of foul medamas, a bean stew with tomatoes, onions, spices, and cheese on the side.

"Thank you so much for making this wonderful meal," I said as I took a seat on one side of the table.

"You are very welcome." She turned to the woman who had opened the door from me and said something in Arabic.

"Maya is going to bring us a drink that I want you to try. If you don't like it, then you can skip it of course, but it's a traditional liqueur made from dates that are grown here in East Africa. You won't be able to find it anywhere else."

"Oh, okay. Sure." I helped myself to a mound of food from the table and began to wolf it down as quickly as basic politeness would allow.

We sipped on the drinks and feasted on the food in silence for the next several minutes.

"I'm going to take your silence as proof that you are enjoying the food, Naina," Mashi said.

"I am," I said, smiling.

She sat back in her chair and started to make conversation again. "So tell me about your fiancé. How long have you been engaged?"

"His name is Dev. It actually has been a few months since he proposed."

"Oh, a formal proposal. What did he do?"

My eyes lit up at the memory. I told her about how Dev took me to the rooftop of our building in the middle of winter and proposed while the snow was coming down around us.

"Were you surprised?" Mashi asked.

"I knew it was a matter of *when* at that point, but I had no idea it would happen at that moment."

"That's so sweet. I'm very happy for the both of you. Do you have a picture of him?"

"Not with me," I answered. "I only brought my travel phone."

"Maybe next time."

The conversation went dead for a moment before Mashi spoke again.

"Naina, there's something I wanted to ask you."

Uh-oh. Here it comes. "Of course."

"Why did you decide to come here?"

I raised my eyebrows, feigning confusion. "I thought I already told you that. I was nearby, so I figured it was time to give it a shot."

"Come on. We both know that there has to be more to this visit than that. You never called or wrote before you showed up here."

I sighed. "I don't know what to tell you, Mashi. Something happened that made me remember you and Nitu, so I decided to try to find you. I wasn't sure if you were still here, so I figured showing up would be the best way to find out if you were."

"You wanted to find Nitu?" she asked. Her hand shook as she put her fork down on the table.

"Yes, I did. I do, rather." My voice dropped to a whisper. "You're the only one who could help me find him."

"But why would you come here to find him? He must still be in India. I'm sure his father would have never moved away."

I shrugged. "He might be, but I have no idea where to look. He could be anywhere." I fiddled with my engagement ring, which I'd worn in direct defiance to your Dida's wishes since the chance of running into an American reporter in East Africa was approximately three hundred thousand to one. "I don't even know his real name. You're the only one who could help me."

Mashi gulped down half of her glass of liqueur. "What exactly do you want from me?"

I crossed my arms and met her eyes directly. "Do you know where Nitu is?"

She shook her head slowly. "Naina, did you have any real interest in finding me, outside of just looking for Nitu?"

My eyes darted around the room. I didn't want to make eye contact with her. "Mashi, I don't know how to answer that question. Of course I had some interest in finding you. I'm here, aren't I? But I didn't get much further than that when I was planning. All I know is that you haven't been a part of my life for the past twenty years."

A glimmer of hope passed across her face. "Do you want that to change?"

"I don't know. I can't answer that question yet. It's too much right now. I feel as if I just met you."

A tear rolled down her cheek. "Okay." She grabbed a piece of paper and a pen from a drawer in the sideboard behind her, scribbled a couple of things down, and placed it on the table in front of me. "That's Nitu's full, legal name and the last address I had for his father, where he was living when I left. That was a long time ago, though."

I picked up the paper and tried to give her a comforting look. "Thank you. Nitu's name is Karan? We didn't even know that much. We only remember Nitu."

"Naina, I have an idea. You're still in Taisoun for another couple of days. Would you spend that time here, in my house? I want the chance to get to know you a little bit. Last time I saw you, you were only eight." She hesitated. "I miss my sister. Your visit has made me realize how much, and you're probably the only connection to her that I will ever have again."

I sighed. The emotions on her face were real, but I felt as if I were fighting through a tidal wave. The deluge made me feel as if I were about to drown. I couldn't look at her face any more. Being alone in the hotel room offered me a last bit of solace. A modicum of independence to swim to the surface. "Why do you want me to stay here?"

"As I said, I want to get to know you. That's all. And I want you to get to know me. I was in a bad place the last time I spoke to your mother. I want you to form your own opinion of the way I am now, not how I used to be." She looked at me with forlorn eyes. "About twenty years ago, I did a terrible thing. I wish I could take it back, but I can't. I can't change the past, but I would like for us to have a future."

I kept my eyes fixed firmly on my hands. I didn't know how to answer her. Sure, she couldn't change the past, but why hadn't she tried to contact any of us? Why didn't she try to be a mother to her son?

"Naina, you came all this way. There must be some part of you that wanted to get to know me. I want you to see me for yourself. And I think you want that too."

"Look, I wouldn't want to impose on you and your husband." I could barely choke out the sentence, let alone the last word. "Why don't I just stay at the hotel for the next few days? I'll visit with you. I promise. Staying here would be too much of an impos—"

"Oh, don't be silly. As if I'd let my own flesh and blood stay at a sterile old hotel instead of my home. You won't be imposing on us in the slightest bit. And what better way for us to get to know you?"

My mind flashed back to a conversation with one of my friends when he had told me how uncomfortable he felt staying in his father's house. His parents were divorced and his father had long since moved through a number of different homes. My friend had asserted repeatedly that his father's home with his new wife felt nothing like his old home. They were warm, friendly, and cordial to him, but he felt an odd formality toward them. I tried to sympathize, but I could never comprehend his emotions. I always thought he was being dramatic until I sat in front of Mashi as she attempted to convince me to stay at her house. Every fiber of my being yearned to return to my impersonal, sterile hotel room.

I was so hesitant to respond that she picked up on my discomfort. "You didn't know about him, did you?" she asked. She'd clearly noticed how my tone had turned icy once again.

"No." I shook my head.

"Tareq really is a wonderful man. I know that he isn't your *Mesho,* or at least, not the one you might remember, but he is my husband." Mashi gave me a lingering stare. "I don't think I should have to justify his existence. The Mesho you remember, things between us didn't work out. I only found a real partner when I met Tareq. He's been wonderful, and we're really happy together."

I examined the diamond pattern of the floor tiles in silence. *Good for you.*

"Come on, Naina. Give him a chance. Don't judge him for what I did. He's a good man, and I want the two of you to get to know each other."

"I can't get to know him when I don't even know you." I gestured with my hands to stop her from interrupting. "I'm not trying to accuse you. You did what you did, and I don't understand it. It's not your husband's fault. I get that. It's just that you moved on from all of us without looking back. We can't bridge that kind of distance in a couple of days."

My chest shook as I exhaled deeply. I tapped my fingers together against the table. "Maybe you're right that we could get to know each other without all of that baggage. I promise I'll think about it." I took a deep breath. "But I can't stay here. That's too much for me. Too much, way too fast."

Her posture shifted and the disappointment in her stance was almost palatable; at least it meant that she would no longer push me on that point. We finished our plates in silence.

I fidgeted in my seat through the rest of the meal. When my plate was successfully emptied, I decided to excuse myself. "If you don't mind, I'd like to get back to the hotel. It's getting late."

She nodded. "There's no chance that I can convince you? You could save a lot of money by staying here."

"No." I stopped myself before the explanation spilled out once again.

"I'll have my driver take you."

Thirty minutes later, I was lying down in my hotel room. The bland, off-white color of the walls and the soulless furniture had never felt so welcoming.

****

April, 2017 – The aftermath of the first encounter

As soon as my eyes opened in the morning, I booted up my tablet to call Dev. "How are you doing?" he asked.

"I don't know," I sighed. It's a weird situation."

"That bad? What happened? Did you go over there?"

"Yeah. It was okay, I guess. We talked about some random stuff. Dinner was really good." I paused, unsure of how to describe the rest of the evening. It was all I had been thinking about for the past twelve hours, but the description now eluded me. *What else could I say?*

"That doesn't sound so bad," he commented. I could tell that he had noticed my hesitation.

"I guess."

"Did you ask her about Nitu?"

"A little bit. She gave me his real name and the last address that she knew of."

"That's good," he said. "Did she say anything else about him?"

"No, that's it. Then she asked me to stay with them."

"Wow. That's a nice gesture. Are you going to do it?"

I shook my head. "I can't do it. That's way too much. I have no idea how to interact with her. I feel like I'm supposed to be angry, and I am, a little bit anyway. But I just feel so distant. Besides, she never wanted to get to know me until I showed up in Taisoun, so why should I make the extra effort to get to know her? I've already made all of the effort."

Dev gave me a sympathetic look. “Babe, I think that’s what she’s trying to do now. You’re just too upset to see that the invitation is her making an effort. She’s trying to get to know you.”

“Whatever. I know you’re right, but I need some space. I couldn’t stay in that house.”

“You know that’s okay, right? You’re not a bad person because you turned her down,” he said with an understanding nod. “So what are you going to do now?”

I picked up the paper with Nitu’s address. “His last address is in Calcutta. I guess I’ll head there at the end of the week.”

“Any chance I could spirit you back home for a visit first?”

“That would be nice.” The thought brought a smile to my face. “I’ll be home soon. I promise.”

“When do you leave Taisoun? Are you going to extend your stay?”

“No, I’ll just leave the day after tomorrow like I planned.”

He frowned. “What are you going to do until then?”

“Well, there are all kinds of things I could do.” My eyes twinkled. “I could go to the spa and get a massage, watch movies, relax. Maybe I’ll visit one of the local markets. I could go eat some more delicious food. It’s so good, Dev. I’m going to look up some East African recipes when I get home.” I shot him a smirk as I continued in a snarky voice. “I could also hang out with an old friend who lives here. Faisal is a wonderful tour guide. Fancy that.”

Dev’s eyes narrowed into little slits on screen. “Very funny. He hasn’t tried to hit on you, has he?”

"Oh, come on. No, he hasn't. He introduced me to the girl he's thinking about proposing to, so no need to worry about that. Try not to be such a jealous husband." I watched his face redden as I teased him.

"Fine, fine, go hang out with Faisal, if he's free. It's better than you wandering all around Taisoun by yourself anyway."

"Oh, thank you so much for your permission."

"Naina, you don't make things easy for me do you?"

"Why would you want that? Who wants a life partner who takes it easy on them?"

"Are you going to see her again?" he asked quietly.

"I don't know."

"Whatever you decide, I'm here for you, okay?"

I gazed at his image, wishing that I could reach out and touch him, lean on his shoulder, feel his arms around me. "Thank you. Dev, I love you."

"I love you too. I can't wait until you're home."

"Me too."

He tilted his head. I could tell that he was trying to get a better read on my emotions. *Difficult through a computer screen.*

"I should probably go now, if that's okay. I have to prep for a meeting," he said.

"Sure. I'll call you tomorrow."

****

The East African sun was beating down on the pavement outside, so I spent most of the day inside within the comforts of air conditioning. After a hearty breakfast, I lazed around and went through the motions of editing a document for work, but my progress was minimal. I was too distracted to focus on it. I watched a couple of TV episodes, spent some time at the gym, and waited for the sun to drop lower in the sky.

By the time twilight set in, I felt as if cabin fever had overwhelmed me completely. I decided to go for a walk since the weather would be bearable. When I exited the lobby, this time I turned east toward Taisoun University. As soon as I set foot on campus, I could feel the buzz—a difference in the atmosphere from the rest of the city. Conversations I overheard had a different tone and the signage on the buildings was a touch bolder. Other parts of the city felt as if they were resigned to their fates. *We have accepted our fate under a military government and the trade embargo.* On campus, everything was different. The energy was palpable; I could reach out and touch it. People were ready to shout out; they wanted to yell and scream to make sure that they were heard. *We will not quietly accept the status quo. We will not accept a government that has caused so much pain.* The pulse was starting to quicken.

I should have realized that it was the first sign—the first symptom of the revolution. The Arab Spring already had struck so many of East Africa's neighbors, yet it seemed unscathed. The energy had only just started to build. While the world remained focused on conflict zones in Darfur and Somalia, we should have redirected some of our attention toward Taisoun. The first glowing embers had sparked into a flickering fire that would infiltrate the city as it grew into a raging inferno.

The atmosphere reminded me of another trip. My aunt and uncle had visited Syria before the start of the revolution movement there. They saw wonderful sites and feasted on great food. While they were there, they said that they could feel the tension that permeated the air of Damascus. What I sensed that day on the university's campus was an earlier stage of the same movement. I didn't feel exactly what they had described, so I didn't pay much attention to it, didn't think about it much after that day. True, that energy was just a precursor to what they saw in Syria, but the winds of change had already descended on East Africa. We just didn't realize it yet.

****

April, 2017 – Leaving East Africa

I spent my last day in Taisoun with Faisal and Arya. It was Friday, so they both had the day off from work. We took advantage of the relative cool to drive out of the city to see the East African pyramids. If you ever have the chance to see them, Nikhil, you absolutely should. I hope that one day I can visit them with you. They may not be part of your blood, but East Africa is very much a part of our family's history.

The pyramids appear all of a sudden—regal monuments that are adrift in a sea of sand dunes, bold figures that face the solitary desert road connecting Taisoun to the western coast of the Red Sea. The sand and the sun beat down on me as I stared up at these lone, timeworn giants with hardly a soul in the vicinity. I'm sure you'll never forget how many times I've railed at Michael Bay for filming the Egyptian pyramids as if the entire city of Cairo did not exist. If he wanted to replace the largest city in the Middle East with three old huts, he might as well have just filmed out there in East Africa.

We spent an hour walking across the grounds before we got back in the car. Faisal was such a sport for driving us out there so that I could see them. I offered to take over and give him a break, but he refused staunchly. "If I must be a chauffeur, let it be for two wonderful women," he mocked.

On the drive back, I contemplated what I would do the next day. I had a ticket from Taisoun to Calcutta for which I would be leaving in the early afternoon to catch my connecting flight to Doha. *Should I call Mashi or not?* It would be Saturday—the second day of the East African weekend—so there was a good chance that she wouldn't be at the hospital. I had no answers for the questions that she had asked me. *Should I just leave it at what I already said?*

As we approached Taisoun from the north, I made a flash decision.

"Faisal, would you mind dropping me off in Om Tais instead of at the hotel?"

He glanced at me with his eyebrows raised. "Are you sure?"

"It's my last night here. I should probably see her again."

"Of course. You'll have a way to get back to the hotel, right?"

"I think so."

"You better call me if you have any issues, okay? I live close by. If you need a ride, I don't want you waiting around for a taxi."

I answered him in a high-pitched voice. "Yes, Dad. I'll call you if I need anything. I promise to be home by curfew."

I should've questioned Faisal's anxiety then, but I assumed he was just being a protective friend who didn't want me out at night, alone, in a strange city.

****

This time I paid little attention to the house itself as I marched up to the gate to ring the bell. I think I was on some kind of adrenaline high. The emotions associated with coming to see her again had probably raised my blood pressure several notches. I could hear my heart pounding in my ears.

The same sari-clad woman came to answer the door and led me inside. The living room was empty, and I took a seat on the sofa. The walls inched closer and closer to me as I waited.

"I was hoping that you would come," Mashi said as she descended the dramatic staircase in the living room.

I gave her a hesitant smile.

As she walked closer, she said, "You look exhausted. And you got some sun. What have you been up to?"

"I went to visit the pyramids with some friends. It was wonderful, but definitely exhausting."

"That's quite a distance for one day. Doesn't it take four hours to get there?"

I shrugged. "I don't think it was that long. It was only two and a half, maybe three hours each way."

"Oh, of course, the new road is ready now. Was it a smooth drive?"

"No complaints."

Mashi walked to the sideboard and poured herself a drink from a small carafe. "This is that liqueur you tried the other day. Would you like some?"

"Sure."

She poured me a glass and handed it to me. She asked some questions about my job and I answered them. I asked about her life in Taisoun. To an outsider, we were getting to know each other. In reality, we were going through conversation topics one by one to avoid topics that were more painful. It was calculated and jerky, rather than natural and flowing. We went back and forth like that for the better part of an hour. By that time, I had consumed a sufficient amount of alcohol. I don't think I was actually drunk or buzzed, but the alcohol gave me enough of an excuse to ask about something I really wanted to know.

"Mashi," I said in a halting voice, "there's something I've been avoiding. Something that I have to ask you. I don't want to make you uncomfortable, but I need to hear the answer. It might be hard for you to talk about. It's even hard for me to talk about, but I still need to know."

I wanted to ask, but I did not want to pry. I wanted to know, but I did not want to see. I wanted to hear, but I did not want to listen. I needed her to speak, but I did not want to understand.

She sighed and nodded with a forlorn expression. She'd obviously been waiting for me to ask about it.

I took a deep breath. "What happened between you and Mesho all those years ago? I've heard different things, from my mom and family gossip, but I want to hear it from you. What made you disappear? Why did you leave?" *Why did you cut all of us off?* I'm sure everyone in my family had asked that question about her disappearance at one time or another. I finally had the opportunity to confront her for the real answer.

She returned to the sideboard and refilled both of our drinks. "I'm going to need some more of this to get through that story." Three gulps later, she started to tell me what I was so curious to know.

"I met Mokul when I was in medical college. He was working at a small café near the campus. He was young and handsome and dashing. He was studying to take his entrance exams, and I was so sure that he would succeed. I was drawn to something about him. Maybe it was how hard he had to work for everything in his life. Mokul was so disciplined with his work. He was going to take a late entrance into college. His school never offered him enough to pass the exams the first time around." She gave me a wistful smile. "He was from such a different background. Your Dadu worked so hard to make sure that we had everything. Your mom and I, and Sameer Mama, we had an easy time. All of our bills were paid and he made sure that we knew how important school was. It was hard on us at first, when he was away finishing his PhD, but when he returned, everything changed. We had a beautiful home, plenty of money, everything that we needed." She threw back her head and drained the glass. "Mokul came from so much less, but he had just as much ambition as I did. We started spending time together. He would make me smile and helped make school more bearable."

She sighed. "He was going to get himself through college and become a mechanical engineer. He believed in himself so much that I believed in him too. But I was wrong."

"Did you ever tell my mom about him?"

"No. Rita had already left India by then, and we didn't talk that often anyway. I'm six years younger than her, so we were never especially close, not like sisters who shared clothes or had the same friends. I tried to bring up Mokul one time when she was visiting, but we couldn't seem to get a moment alone."

I took a deep breath. "I see."

"Before I graduated, I told him that he had to speak to my parents. He had just taken the entrance exams again. I wanted to get married, and I didn't want to wait until he received his test results," Mashi said.

"Why?"

"I knew that *Baba* had already started looking at a potential match for me. He even showed me some pictures, and we talked about some different men he wanted me to meet."

"Dadu wanted you to have an arranged marriage?" I interjected.

Mashi shook her head. "No. Your mom didn't have one and neither did our brother. He just wanted to set me up, see if I clicked with anyone, play matchmaker. Back then, it was unusual for a girl who was almost twenty-five to be unattached. Since I never told my parents about Mokul, I can't blame them for wanting to introduce me to a few people."

"But you did finally tell them about him."

"Yes, of course. Mokul spoke to them, and Baba canceled the set-up with some guy he really wanted me to meet. The two of us were married soon after that. We were happy and in love." This time when she spoke, her voice was trembling. "And I had just found out that I was pregnant."

"Wow. I, I had no idea that Nitu was born so soon after you were married."

Her hands shook as she refilled her glass. "He wasn't. I had a, a miscarriage."

I bit down on my lip. "I'm so sorry."

Mashi nodded. "It happened about a month after we were married. Right before Mokul received his results."

"Did you ever tell my mom about it? Or anyone else?" I probed. This would probably be my only chance to find out the answers to these questions, and I wanted to take advantage of the opportunity. Some part of me also knew that I would have to answer these questions myself when my mother heard that I had found Mashi. Once I found Nitu, I figured he would probably want answers as well.

"No. I was too embarrassed to tell her that I was pregnant when I got married."

"What happened then?"

"A couple of weeks after…he received his results."

I frowned. "And?"

"He failed his tests. I guess those two things, well, that's when everything started to go wrong."

"Did he try again?"

"No. I think he was too scared. He didn't want to fail again."

"Why?"

She sighed. "I don't know, Naina. At some point, we stopped being able to talk about things. I guess he decided it wasn't worth the effort." She took a slow deep breath. "I'm sure he would have passed if he had tried again, but I didn't know how to talk to him anymore. He was resentful that I had to earn all of our money, and honestly, so was I."

"Is it true then? That you were the family breadwinner?"

"Yes. Mokul was, and I'm sure still is, a wonderful man. But he could never earn enough to support us as a family."

I could see the pain on her face. So many years later and she still carried those memories. She looked as if she were recounting something that had just happened to her. "When did you start to realize that you would have to take care of everything?"

"Subconsciously, I probably knew right after he failed his entrance exams. Consciously, I don't know. I started to feel more and more like a prisoner in the house a few months into it. I was working crazy hours, double shifts at the hospital to pay the bills and take care of the house, all while I was doing my postgraduate course in general surgery. Mokul did his best to help, but he could only add so much to our bank account by waiting tables. I was pregnant again, and I'm sure my hormones only made things worse."

"When was Nitu born?" I asked.

"A year and a half after we were married. Things were pretty bad at that point. We argued all the time. Things became even worse about halfway through my pregnancy. I'd been working so hard and I wanted to slow down for the baby. I was scared of having another miscarriage, and I couldn't imagine going through that again. I didn't know how we could afford to have a baby. Some days I felt as if the walls were closing in on me." Mashi shrugged. "After Nitu was born, it didn't get any better either. A few years later, I really couldn't handle it anymore. It was all too much, so I, I…"

"You decided to leave."

"Yes."

I crossed my arms. "How old was Nitu at that point?"

"It was just after his sixth birthday."

"Six years old?" The casual way in which she mentioned the age of her son when she had abandoned him struck me to the core. I couldn't remember that much from when I was six, but I knew that my mother was essential to my existence.

"How could you do that?" I gaped. "You left your six-year-old son because you were arguing with your husband all the time? Why couldn't you just get a divorce? You could have left Mesho without abandoning Nitu."

"You're right, but a friend of mine told me I could be stuck in divorce paperwork for over a year. At the time, well, a year felt like another eternity. I didn't know how to get through another day trapped within those walls. So I just took off." Several tears trickled down Mashi's face. "To this day, I don't fully understand why I left Nitu. I did eventually figure out that I was depressed, and nobody thinks clearly with that clouding the mind. Anxiety and exhaustion and depression drove me toward some terrible choices. Leaving was self-preservation, fight or flight. I didn't have any fight left in me, so I fled. I know it was incredibly selfish, but I felt so alone and just wanted to save myself. I wish I could change it, do things differently." She paused and looked up at the ceiling in an effort to ebb the flow of tears.

"But I can't," she whispered. "I just figured, or hoped, that it would be better for Nitu, without his parents fighting all the time. I didn't even know where I was going or what I was going to do, and I didn't want to drag Nitu into that craziness. So leaving him with his father, in the only home he had ever known, it made sense in my mind. It doesn't now, but it did then, it did for years." She shut her eyes.

Yes, because being abandoned has no impact on a child, I wanted to say. I held my tongue and let the reaction subside. "Did you ever try to contact Nitu again?"

"No," she coughed out between sobs. "I didn't know if he'd want to hear from me. I didn't know if Mokul would allow it. And I knew Nitu had to hate me anyway. The depression faded, but that fear and shame has always remained."

I rubbed my eyes and stared down at the floor. "I'm sure that he does want to hear from you. He might be angry or distant…but I bet that he'd still want to hear from you."

"I'm sure that they're both fine," she choked.

I swallowed loudly as I remembered the conversation about Nitu and his father that I'd heard when I was a teenager in Calcutta. "I'm not sure it was that easy for them, that it all turned out okay," I said before I could stop myself.

Her face turned ashen. "What do you mean?"

"It doesn't matter."

"Please, Naina."

"I overheard a conversation once. I don't remember exactly when. I was probably fifteen or so."

"What did you hear?"

"Mom and I were in the car with Sameer Mama when Mesho called. He said things were desperate for them. That he didn't know how to take care of Nitu. That they didn't have any money and he needed help."

"He did?" Her lower lip trembled.

"Yes."

"What did Sameer say?"

I swallowed slowly. "He said to bring Nitu to them. They would take care of him."

"So Mokul took Nitu to Sameer's home?" Her eyes were still tearful, but they brightened as she looked at me. "You said you didn't know where Nitu was now, but he was at Sameer's back then?"

"No."

"What do you mean?"

"I don't know what happened. They never showed. Sameer Mama tried to find them, but he couldn't. We never heard from them after that. Never again."

Mashi's torso began to shake uncontrollably.

I sat there, frozen. My first instinct was to comfort her, but something rendered me immobile. We had bridged some of the distance between us just by having the conversation, but part of me didn't want to comfort her. *She deserves to feel some of that pain. After all of those years.* The gap between us had been closing, but with the blink of an eye, she seemed even further away than before.

I watched her shiver until she reached out and grabbed my hand. The single touch was enough to change everything. In front of me was a woman torn up by her guilt. She had done a terrible thing, and she deserved to suffer. What scared me was that I had no answers for her. If I'd known for sure that Nitu was okay, I could have let her suffer, and only ended her pain at my discretion. It made me feel sick that I considered letting her suffer simply because I thought it was just, and I struggled with what to do. I could comfort her, but I could not offer any solace. Finally, I could stand it no longer. I squeezed her hand and tried to make eye contact. "Mashi, I'm going to find him." My voice projected so much more confidence than I felt.

Her face immediately perked up. She opened her mouth to say something and closed it again. "Will you promise me something? When you find him…will you bring him here? I want to meet him. I want to see him."

My mouth fell open. How could she ask me to promise that? I might never even find him, but even if I did, I couldn't force him to come to East Africa. "Well…"

"Please, Naina. You said yourself that he might be angry and distant, but he might still want to see me, to see his mother again."

That's not exactly what I said, I remember thinking. With her tears still fresh, though, I could not shatter her hopes. *I'm going to regret this,* I thought as I nodded my ascent.

"When you come back, you should stay a few days. Stay here. I'd like to get to know you as well."

I took a deep breath. "I'm not sure if I'm ready for that."

Her eyes were deep and sad as she asked me, "What kind of relationship do you want to have with me?"

I didn't have an answer for her. I shook my head as I tried to come up with one and mumbled my previous response. "I still don't know yet." Then I bolted before I could make any other promises that I wouldn't be able to keep.

****

The next morning, I took a shuttle from the hotel with my bags in hand. I was still mulling over the question that Mashi had asked me. I glanced at my phone and even picked it up to dial her number, but put it down when I could not think of the right words to say. As the driver sped past the university, I threw caution to the wind.

"Hi, Mashi. It's Naina calling," I said as she picked up.

"I'm so glad you called. How are you?"

"I'm fine. I'm on my way to the airport now."

"Of course," she sighed. "You did say you were leaving today."

I took a deep breath and forced out the words. "I wanted to talk to you before I left. Look, I still don't know how to answer your question about what kind of relationship I want with you. I barely know anything about you, and it's not enough to decide what kind of relationship we can have. I just don't know. There is one thing I wanted to tell you, though. I am glad that I came. And not just for Nitu."

"I understand," she said with a sniffle. "Thank you for calling me."

"Wait, there's more. There has to be a reason why I found you. I don't want to leave now and never speak to you again. Like I said, I don't know what kind of relationship I want with you, but I am willing to try to find out."

I could hear the shocked gratitude in her voice when she answered, "That's, that's great."

"Let's just take things slowly. I want to try to get to know you, and I want you to try to get to know me. I'll do my best to open up. One conversation at a time. Okay?" I could hear my pulse pounding in my ears as I waited for her to respond.

"Yes, of course."

"Good."

"Have a safe flight. Give me a call sometime when you're ready?"

"I will, Mashi."

"And Naina, don't worry about that other thing, okay?"

"Sure," I whispered. Relief washed over me. *At least I don't have to convince Nitu to come to East Africa with me.* I wasn't even sure I wanted to return myself. All I could hope for in that moment was that I would be able to find him. If I'd only realized then how naïve my thought process was.

The phone clicked shut, and I leaned back into the car seat. A weight had been lifted off my shoulders. I knew that I had done the right thing, no matter what feelings I had or would have about Mashi. I was nowhere near being able to answer her question about our relationship, and I still had no idea how I would explain what had happened to my mom. Part of me wanted to keep it a secret, which certainly would have been the easiest option. As you already know, though, the easy path isn't always the right one. I could never lie to Mom about what had just happened. I knew that in every fiber of my being, just as I knew that we could no longer keep this secret from you with your own child on the way. I'm sorry if we waited too long. We wanted to be sure that you could understand without judgment, but that became an easy justification for our own fear. It was easier to put it off than to bring ourselves to tell you. We can only hope that you handle this with the same grace that you did when we told you that you were adopted. At the time, we assured you that you are our son in everything but blood.

But, Nikhil, the truth is that you are my blood. We haven't talked about Nitu much, but you've seen a few of his pictures in our old photo albums. I think you even overheard Mashi say that you look like him once, when she visited us in Paris when you were a teenager. That's true—you do bear an uncanny resemblance to him. You have the same nose, and the cut of your features is almost a carbon copy. It's no coincidence that when I hear you laugh, I can feel his presence too.

I left East Africa for Calcutta to look for Nitu. When I found him, I also found you, his only son.

****

April, 2017 – My search in Calcutta

I arrived in Calcutta early the next morning and took a taxi to my family's apartment in the South City complex. It took me a minute to wiggle the lock open. Once I did, I dumped my bags and went out onto the balcony.

The view from the twenty-eighth floor was amazing. I could see the grassy grounds of the complex framed by major Calcutta landmarks, including the Victoria Memorial and Salt Lake. The city seemed vibrant and buzzing. As I took in the view, I wondered if Nitu was still living there. I'd stuffed the address Mashi had given me into my purse. I dug it out and read it for the hundredth time. I had memorized it by then, but the piece of paper made it seem all the more real, especially since the last address I could recall for him was in Bombay, not Calcutta.

I made my way back inside and pulled out my computer to put a call through to Dev.

"Hi, sweetie," he said with a smile when his image appeared on my screen.

"Hi. How are you, my love?"

"I'm okay. I miss you."

"I miss you too."

He tilted his head to the side. "So you're in the South City apartment? I can't believe that I still haven't been there."

"Yeah. It's not in great condition at the moment, though. How about we postpone the tour until you can see it in person? After the renovation."

"Fine," he grumbled and crossed his arms. "How come it's not in great condition? I thought your uncle usually sets it up for you."

I pursed my lips. "I, er, I didn't tell Sameer Mama that I was coming. Otherwise, he would have sent someone over to set everything up. Normally, he even makes sure that the fridge is stocked with basics, but there's a grocery store in the complex, so don't worry. I'll be fine."

Dev frowned. "How come you didn't tell them that you were coming?"

"I don't know. I didn't want to explain everything, or give them any false hopes about finding Nitu. I want to give it a try before I have to tell them everything."

He rolled his eyes. "Did you at least tell any of your friends that you're there? I don't love the idea of you running around Calcutta all by yourself."

"I spoke to Vijay and Mamta on my way in."

"Okay. Please take one of them with you when you start visiting all of these apartments."

"Dev, I'll be fine. This isn't Kabul or Nairobi."

"I know, but I don't want you doing this alone. You told me that the address you had was basically in the slums. I don't want you going out there by yourself."

I shot him a look. "Dude, you know I'm kidding right? Of course I'm not going there by myself. I'd get totally lost. Mamta and I are going to check it out this afternoon. She's picking me up in a couple hours."

"Oh, well, that's great." His eyes narrowed at me. "Anyway, did you think about my suggestion?"

"Suggestion? You mean to hire a private investigator?"

"Yes."

I shrugged my shoulders. "I can at least go there and visit the apartment on my own. If there are no leads, I can always hire a PI then. Let's just see how it goes today."

"It might get you home sooner."

"It might," I said with a grin. "And it might not. Try not to worry so much." I glanced at my watch. "Anyway, I should go now. I need to get some groceries and make this apartment feel more habitable before Mamta gets here."

"Good. I love you."

"Love you too."

After hanging up, I turned my attention to cleaning up the apartment. It was furnished sparsely with a basic bed and dresser in each of the four bedrooms, two of which were more enlarged dens than bedrooms. There was a sofa and two chairs in the living area with a TV, and a dining room table and chairs next to the small kitchen. Basic kitchen items needed to be resupplied, so a quick trip to the grocery store at the South City Mall remedied that situation. I stocked up the fridge and then collapsed onto the couch to kick my feet up for a few minutes. I was almost asleep when my phone rang.

"Hi, Mamta," I said in a groggy voice.

"Hey, Naina," she said in a sprightly voice. As usual, she spoke at a mile a minute. "Hey! I'm on my way. Should be there in about twenty minutes depending on traffic. Can't wait to see you. I can't believe you're here all of a sudden—"

"Okay, great. See you soon…" My eyes started to close before I'd even hung up the phone.

I sat there for almost ten minutes before I was ready to fight off my exhaustion. When I finally got up, I went through the motions of a rushed shower and scrambled to get dressed. I had just finished getting ready when the doorbell rang.

"Hi," she squealed as I opened the door. She squished me in a hug and her energy started to rub off on me.

"How are you?" I asked as she took a seat on the couch. "What can I get for you? I only have tea and orange juice, unfortunately. And water."

She joined me in the kitchen while I made some tea, and we reminisced about some of our old college memories. After the second cup, we decided to head out. Mamta waited until we reached her car in the parking lot to ask me about where we were going.

"So, Naina, where are we headed? Are we going to see someone? Or is it a shop? Did you want to buy something in particular while you're here?"

"Right." I stopped at the car door as I gathered my thoughts. In all of the excitement, I'd forgotten that I had yet to explain the situation to her. "We are—we're going to see someone," I enunciated each word slowly.

She cocked her head to the side. "What do you mean?"

"It's kind of a long story, and I'd rather tell you the details when we get back. I'm a little nervous about it, and I'd probably tell the story better after we make this little trip. Basically, I'm looking for a relative. My family lost touch with him a long time ago. One of my cousins, he was just a little boy the last time we saw him."

"Wow. That does sound like quite a story." She held my gaze for a moment. I could tell that she wanted to probe further, but she had decided to wait. "Okay, well, get in the car and let's go check it out. You can tell me all about it over dinner later."

She drove us to the address in the old Khidirpur district of Calcutta.

****

It took us an hour to find the particular flat within the slum area. The neighborhood was organized in block numbers. Finding the address should have been a simple affair, but the numbers did not necessarily fall in order. We wandered around asking people where it would be. We also tried inquiring after the Chatterjee's apartment. It was a long shot, especially with such a common surname, and that strategy failed us more than once. Like most areas in Bengal, every third apartment contained at least one Chatterjee. Eventually, we gave up on that and focused exclusively on the address. Finally, we found someone who gave us reliable instructions. He told us to walk through the compound, take a left after the tobacco shop, and turn right when we got to the *pan walla*.

After following those directions, we were able to locate the flat number. I knocked on the door and we waited. A little girl answered the door and stared at us with big eyes.

"Ke khujcho?" she asked, looking us up and down curiously. *Who are you looking for?*

"Apnar ma othobar baba achen?" I said softly. *Are either of your parents here?*

Before she could answer my question, a middle-aged woman appeared behind her. "May I help you?" she asked in Bengali.

"Didi, I'm looking for Karan or Mokul Chatterjee." I showed her the paper with the address. "A man and his son. I believe they used to live here."

She shook her head. "I don't know them."

My heart sank into my stomach. "Did you meet the people who lived here before you?"

"No, my father is the one who moved us here."

"Is he here? Would it be all right if I spoke with him? I'm trying to find my brother."

Mamta looked at me in surprise, and I nudged her so that she wouldn't give away my half-truth.

The woman looked at me questioningly. I could tell that she was debating about letting two strangers into her home. "He doesn't really speak to strangers anymore."

"Please," I implored. "We grew up together, but I haven't seen him in over ten years."

The woman gave me a once-over and sighed. "Just for a few minutes." She stepped aside and led us through the apartment, if it could be called that. It was a series of freestanding rooms built from concrete that were connected by an outdoor path. They had constructed a makeshift roof over the path to turn it into a hallway, but I could tell that it must leak terribly during the rainy season. Mamta eyed me as we walked, and I knew that I would have to tell her the whole story once we were back in the car. There would be no waiting for dinner now to explain everything.

We passed two separate concrete structures before the woman led us through a doorway into the third. Inside, an old man sat on a rocking chair. The only other furniture in the room was a single bed with a mosquito net set up over it. There were three pictures on the wall, including one of a young couple to whom the woman leading us bore a remarkable resemblance. The second picture was an older version of the woman from the other picture. Her face was marked with age and a bright orange marigold garland encircled the frame.

The woman walked up to her father and whispered something to him. He nodded and she turned toward us. "You may speak to him for a couple of minutes." With that, she turned and left the room.

"Daduji," I said, addressing him in Bengali as an elder with respect. "I need your help. I'm looking for my brother. I think he used to live here. Do you remember who was living here before you moved in?"

The elderly man spoke gently. He had a faraway look in his eyes. "We came here when my *nathi* was born. He turned thirteen four months ago. You probably met his little sister. She loves answering the door. Amira *jan* was still with us back then." He gestured toward the picture encircled by the garland.

I listened patiently as he told us how he and his wife were both healthy and more active at that time. They moved into the apartment with his son and daughter-in-law back then. I made note of some of the details in the back of my mind. *They moved here thirteen years ago.* He told us about how he and his son moved their pictures and smaller possessions on a scooter they borrowed from a local bike shop, and recounted how he'd repaired the rain shed that covered the hallway. When he stopped to take a breath, I asked him about Nitu once again.

"Daduji, who was living here before you found this place?"

"There was a young man and his son here. They were struggling to pay the rent, so they needed to move somewhere else. I remember talking to him about it. He was worried about his son, wanted to make sure that he could go to school."

"How old was the boy?" I bit down on my lip to stop my emotions from surfacing.

"I don't know exactly. Maybe eleven or twelve? He can't have been much older than that."

"Do you remember their names?" My heart was racing. It was the closest I'd come to a real connection.

"Chatterjee, I think."

"Do you know where they went after this?"

The old man shook his head. "The man said he had found someone who would help him take care of the boy so that he could take a construction job. He said he needed someone to take care of the boy while he would be at work."

I took in a gulp of air. The timing lined up. That conversation that I had overheard in the car during that trip to Calcutta. I must have been about fifteen at the time, which would put Nitu at twelve. The time when his dad called my uncle asking—no, begging—for help. But what had happened? Why had he never shown up with Nitu?

The trail was about to go cold, but I made one last-ditch effort. "Do you remember anything about the job that he took? Where it was? Anything at all?"

He closed his eyes. I could tell that he was searching his memories. "I think it was that big new apartment complex with the mall. I don't remember the name."

Mamta looked at me startled. "Do you mean South City?" she blurted out.

"Yes, yes that's it," he agreed. "South City. Yes, that's it exactly."

A shiver passed over me. My family had owned a flat at South City since the complex had opened more than nine years ago. It was a huge lead, so part of me wanted to rejoice, but the other part left me feeling repulsed. *He's been so close by for so long.*

"Do you remember anything else about them, Daduji?" Mamta chimed in after she must have noticed my stricken expression.

"The boy's daak nam." *The boy's nickname.*

"Yes?"

"It started with an N. Maybe Nimbu or something similar."

"Nitu?"

He smiled. "Yes, that's it. Nitu."

"That's him. Thank you, Daduji," I said as I reached down to touch the old man's feet in respect.

"God be with you," he said as I stepped away.

I nodded and we made our exit in silence.

****

April, 2017 – A stroke of luck

We pulled into the South City parking lot and Mamta followed me upstairs to the apartment. She hadn't said a word during the drive back about what had transpired.

I shut the door behind me, and we both sat on the couch. "Why don't I get us something to drink?" I said hastily before she could say anything.

I made us two cups of tea and carried them to the living room. I sank down into my seat and sighed. "I'm sorry I didn't tell you more about what you were driving me into."

Mamta crossed her arms. "How about you stop stalling and just tell me now?"

"Okay." I took a long sip of my tea and set the cup down.

"Well?"

"I don't know where to start. I don't think we ever talked about any of this, but my mom has a younger sister."

"Yeah?" Mamta raised her eyebrows.

"When I was a kid, Mashi had a son. He's about three years younger than me." I leaned back into the couch. "I haven't seen him in over twenty years."

"Nitu…"

"Exactly," I said. "Mashi abandoned them when he was only six. We heard from her a couple of times after that, thought she was in East Africa at the time, but we never found her, never heard from her again. We only heard from Nitu's dad once, at least as far as I know. He called to say he didn't have any money and that he was struggling to take care of Nitu by himself. My mom's family offered to help them, but they never showed up, and we could never find them after that."

"Do you mean—what the old man was saying about them leaving their apartment? You think that's when he called?"

"Yeah, I think so."

"Wow."

We sipped on our tea in silence. I had no idea what else to say. Should I tell her about the trip to East Africa? About the background check? Or just switch gears and start talking about wedding planning? We hadn't seen each other in almost three years, and I wasn't sure how open I could be about complicated family issues.

Then Mamta broke the silence in a way that I could never have imagined. "Vijay and I are separated."

It took all of my self-control to keep my jaw from falling open in shock. "What? When? What happened?"

"He had an affair…"

"Oh my God." I reached out and put my arms around her. Her torso shook slightly and I released her. "Mamta, when did this happen? Were you guys having problems? How did you find out?"

She shrugged. "Things haven't been working for a long time. I guess everything started to go downhill once our honeymoon period wore off." She shook her head. "I never thought that we got married too quickly, but now I wonder if that's what we did wrong."

Her teacup was shaking in her quivering hand. I took it from her and placed it on the coffee table. "I'm so sorry. Are you okay?"

"It was worse when I first found out. I knew things weren't going well, but I never imagined it was something like this. He gave me the login to his computer one morning because mine had crashed and I needed to work. He'd left his e-mail open, and a message was right there. I just caught a glimpse of it when I was about to close the window, from some girl who works with a supplier. She said that she couldn't wait to see him again and how they'd had such a good time last time he visited." Tears began to roll down Mamta's cheeks.

The optimist in me wanted to believe it was a misunderstanding, even if I knew she was right. "Did you talk to him about it?"

She shook her head. "No. I was so angry and upset that I took my wedding ring off and went out to a club that night with Chetan."

Nooo. My eyes widened as I stifled my initial reaction. "You went out with Chetan? Oh, Mamta." I grasped her hand and squeezed it. "I thought you stopped speaking to him after we graduated. God, he screwed you over, broke your heart. It took you years to get over him. It's been five or six years since you guys split the first time. Please don't tell me you're going back to him—"

"I know, I know. I don't know what came over me."

I swallowed loudly. "Did something happen? With Chetan?"

She gave me such a slight nod that I almost missed it.

"Oh, Mamta." I wrapped my arms around her again in an even tighter hug. "Do you want to talk about it?"

"He took me home, and I let him into the house. He kissed me, but when he started taking my clothes off, I threw him out."

Internally, I let out a huge sigh of relief. *Thank God.* I'd lost count of how many times I'd helped Mamta off the floor because Chetan had broken her heart yet again, and I'd even wondered if she was over him when she and Vijay first started dating.

"There's more, Naina. I'm pregnant."

This time my jaw did drop open. "Shit," I cursed quietly.

"*Shit* is right," she said, forcing a smile.

I put my arm around her and rubbed her shoulder. "Have you told Vijay yet?"

"No."

"Mamta, when are you going to tell him?"

"I don't know."

I sighed. "Does he know about Chetan? That you saw him again?"

"I haven't told him, but I'm sure he knows that something happened. There were people at the club that night who know both of us. Vijay's probably heard some gossip by now."

"And you haven't told him about the e-mail you found?"

"No." She crossed her arms and looked toward the ceiling. "I couldn't bring myself to say anything. I didn't want to hear him try to lie his way out of it. I just want to run away."

I frowned, confused. "If you didn't tell him you found that message, and he doesn't know about Chetan…what did he say to you before he moved out? Have you two talked about anything at all?"

Her shoulders convulsed. "He called me from Bombay the day before yesterday and said that he wasn't coming home. He was going to stay out there and take some time to think. He didn't think things were working out between us." She leaned her head back against the wall. "He said we needed to figure out a way to tell our families that we were splitting up."

I gaped at her with a blank expression. What could I say? I reached out and rubbed her shoulder softly. She leaned into me and sobbed onto my shoulder as I tried to gather my thoughts. I remembered reading somewhere that divorce was one of the most stressful events that could occur in someone's life, superseded only by the death of a spouse.

We didn't talk much more after that. We sat around and watched two movies in a row on my computer later that night. Neither of us was interested in dinner after the day we had. Without her saying so, I knew that Mamta would be staying over. I made up one of the beds, but it turned out to be unnecessary. She was passed out on the couch by the time I returned from the bedroom. I covered her up with a blanket and went into my bedroom to call Dev on Skype video chat.

"Hey," he exclaimed. "I didn't think you'd call until tomorrow. How did it go?"

I sighed. "We found Nitu's old place, but they don't live there anymore. I talked to the old man who lives there now. He thinks that Nitu's dad took a job with a construction crew here at South City. That might be enough of a lead to keep looking."

"I think you should hire a PI."

It took me a moment to acknowledge that he was right. I had reached the limit of what I could do on my own. "Yeah, I think you're right. I'll start looking into it tomorrow."

He frowned. "Babe, what's wrong? Are you okay? This is good news. It's a huge lead. You're going to find him."

"I know. It's Mamta. Vijay's been having an affair and they're probably going to get divorced. I've known them for forever, so it just makes me sad."

"I'm sorry. I know you've always been close to both of them."

"It just sucks, you know? Now I have to choose a side, and I was close to both of them way before they got together."

"I'm giving you a big, big hug," he said with a sympathetic look.

"I know," I said, blinking rapidly. "Thanks."

"You should go and get some rest. Try not to think too much. Something good will happen in the next couple of days. I'm sure of it."

He couldn't have been more right. At the time, all I could see was how broken marriage had made some people's lives. I wasn't afraid of my upcoming marriage; I was just becoming more aware of how quickly things could fall apart. I sat down in the living room next to where Mamta had passed out. My body was exhausted, but my mind was awake and fixated on the events of the day. After she tossed and turned a couple of times, I tried in vain to get her to bed.

Eventually, I let her be on the couch and went to snuggle under the covers in my room. I lay on my back and wondered what made some marriages work and others fail. A friend of mine once said that a relationship needs the three Cs: chemistry, compatibility, and circumstance. When you reached the point of marriage, which of those became the most important?

Now that your father and I have been married for thirty years, I would add communication as the fourth C that surpasses all of the rest. That being said, the original three are still incredibly important. I'm writing this here, Nikhil, because I want to make sure that you consider the importance of those factors. If you do decide to marry Kanika, make sure that you are truly ready. There were times when I faulted Dev for taking so long to propose to me, but I'm so glad now that he took his time. When we said our vows in front of our families, and in front of you, we were both more than ready to take that step. We took our time to discover what marriage meant to each of us so that we could handle the obstacles that life has thrown our way.

That first night in Calcutta, I fell asleep dreaming about marriage as an institution. The next morning I awoke to the smell of fresh *luchis* and roasted vegetables.

"Mamta, you didn't need to make breakfast," I exclaimed. I was still in my pajamas when I greeted her in the kitchen, while she was already dressed and hard at work.

She shot me a glance. "It's the least I can do for unloading on you last night."

I saw the rolling pin in her hand and stepped away with a grin. "Don't be silly. That's what friends are for." I grabbed a fresh *luchi* from the top of the pile next to the wok full of hot oil, tore a bite off, and popped it into my mouth. "That being said, you can cook for me anytime."

"Why thank you," Mamta said with a short laugh. "You have to wait until the vegetables are ready." She swatted my hand away from the pile of steaming flatbreads.

As I kept munching on the one that I had already stolen, I was struck by her ability to remain upbeat even when the worst was raining down on her. She's always been that way, even when we were just nineteen-year-olds trying to make it through our next exam.

"I have something else for you." She motioned toward her purse. There was a single business card leaning against it.

The card read, "Pritham Maitra, Private Investigator," with a phone number and address in Calcutta.

"Where did you get this?" I frowned as I turned the card in my hand a couple of times.

"I hired him to confirm what I saw in Vijay's e-mails. That was before I called Chetan. I didn't want Vijay to have an easy way out. I was worried that he would make the whole thing go away, seem like nothing."

"I see." My eyes moved between her face and the business card. "And did he confirm what you saw in the e-mail?"

Her hands shook as she placed a bowl of piping hot food on the table. "Yes," she whimpered.

"I'm so sorry, Mamta."

She wiped her eyes quickly and sat down in front of me. "He only confirmed what I already knew. Anyway, you should call him today. He's a good investigator, so I'm sure he'll be able to find your cousin. I don't think we'll be able to do much on our own. I know you hate the idea of hiring someone but—"

"Mamta—"

"Naina, I only want to hear that you'll call him as soon as we finish breakfast. You don't need to do everything on your own."

"But I—"

Mamta shook her finger at me dramatically, and we both cracked up.

"I was trying to say that I agreed with you," I protested. "Last night, I told Dev that I would look for a PI. I would have told you that if you hadn't assumed that I would disagree."

She moved her head from side to side in a sassy display. "Hmm, well, I'm sure he's been working on that for days if he got you to agree."

I rolled my eyes. "Okay, you're right, he has."

"Exactly. You're the most independent-minded creature I have ever met. You always want to do everything by yourself."

"I am not going to respond to that," I said haughtily as I helped myself to some of the fried flatbread luchis along with the vegetable *sabji*.

Thirty minutes later, I called the private detective. I gave him the information I had over the phone along with how to reach me. He promised to get back to me within the next couple of days. Tentatively, we set up an appointment for the end of the week.

****

"Here's the information you requested," Pritham Maitra said in Bengali as he handed me a slim file. "There's background on both Mokul and Karan Chatterjee. I identified them using the address you provided along with the information about South City. We're still compiling current information on both of them. You'll have it in the next couple of days."

I nodded as I glanced through the file. The first two pages were about my uncle. After working on the South City construction project, he worked on two other construction sites in different parts of Calcutta. My heart sank as I read that he had passed away four years earlier. *Poor Nitu.* At the age of twenty-five, he'd already lost both of his parents.

I skipped to the description of my cousin. "Is this a current picture?" My breath caught as I spoke and it came out in a hushed tone, not quite a whisper.

"Yes, but we'll have something more recent for you in a few days. That picture could be up to five years old. It's the picture in the government database, from his license."

"And this address. That means he's still here? In Calcutta?"

The PI nodded. "We'll have more details for you later this week, but as far as we know, yes."

"What about the phone number?" I asked.

"We're still trying to get a cell phone number. That number belongs to the address."

"Okay. Once you have more information, please give me a call. As soon as you get confirmation on that address, I'd like to see him as soon as possible." My emotions were running amuck and a wave of dizziness passed over me on my way back to the apartment. *Just a few more days.*

****

After I left the private investigator's office, I clung to the piece of paper from the file as if my life depended on it. *Just pick up the phone and call the number.* I was frozen, paralyzed. I might actually have found Nitu, but fear held me back. *This address hasn't even been confirmed.* I justified my feelings over and over.

I turned on my computer and dialed Dev's number in France.

"Hey, sweetie," he said as his image appeared on screen.

"Hi," I sighed.

"What's the matter?"

"I'm not sure what to do. I just keep staring at this file the PI gave me."

Dev raised his eyebrows. "Didn't he give you an address?"

"He did. But it's not confirmed."

"So you're just waiting?"

"Yeah."

"Naina, go and check out the address."

"Are you sure? Maybe I should wait for confirmation."

"What's the worst that could happen? You have nothing to lose by checking out another place. You don't even have to go to the door if you aren't ready to do that."

I shrugged my shoulders. "I don't know. I don't want to get my hopes up again. I guess they're already up. I just don't want to be disappointed again."

"Babe, waiting is going to drive you crazy. Go. Just don't go alone."

"Don't worry. I'll take one of my friends with me."

"Preferably one of the guys, please. I can't believe you went wandering around the slums with just Mamta." His expression was stern.

"Oh, come on. Mamta is a tough cookie. And it was in the middle of the day," I protested. "Okay. I'll be safe. Don't worry. We'll have Mamta's manly driver take us this time."

Later that evening, we parked in front of the address identified in the file.

That's when everything changed.

****

A young woman answered the door. Just beyond her, a little boy squatted over a set of Lego blocks. That was the first time that I saw you.

"Baba, some people are here!" you called out as she opened the door.

"Coming, *beta*," I heard from somewhere in the background.

Nitu has a son?

A young man came to the door with dark brown hair and eyes. He stood at about five-foot-eight and appeared to be in his midtwenties. "Thank you, Sita," he said to the woman who had answered. She disappeared into the kitchen, and he turned toward us. "Hi. May I help you?"

I looked him over, trying to discern if he could be Nitu. I'd seen the photo in the file, but in that moment, my mind was completely blank. I could no longer remember the person in the photo. I racked my brain for any specific features, but came up short. We stood there in silence for so long that Mamta spoke up for me.

"Hi. We're sorry to bother you. We're looking for a Karan Chatterjee," she said.

The young man pursed his lips. "You've found him. How can I help you?"

I bit down on my lip in an attempt to muster the words. "Er, are you the son of Mokul Chatterjee and Trina Banerjee? Formerly of this address?" I held out the original note with the information that Mashi had given me.

He frowned as he examined the note. "Yes, I believe so. That's me. How did you get this address?"

I didn't want to tell him that Mashi had given me the address because I didn't know how he would react to me being in touch with his mother. I took a deep breath and said the first thing that popped into my mind. "I think my mother visited you there once. Before you moved to Bombay."

"Your mother? But we gave up that address over thirteen years ago."

"Back when you were a kid."

His posture stiffened. "Who are you?"

"I don't know how much you remember. I'm Rita Mashi's daughter, Naina." My right hand shook as I extended it to shake his hand.

He blinked rapidly. "I guess you'd better come in, Naina didi."

****

April, 2017 – Nitu and you

The ceiling fan clattered overhead as Nitu and I both avoided eye contact. The furnishings of his apartment became far more interesting as I searched for inspiration on how to start a conversation.

The woman who had answered the door handed us small cups of tea and asked Nitu for permission to leave. He nodded and she left. I focused on stirring the tea as I peered down the hallway to where you were playing with your Lego blocks. Mamta had already gone over to you and was helping you build a tower on top of a toy truck.

Nitu finally broke the silence. "So, er, how is Rita Mashi?" he asked.

"She's very well."

"I wish she had come with you. I remember that she was very sweet to me."

A smile crossed my face. "How long have you been living here?"

"A couple of years. What about you? Where do you live now?"

"My fiancé and I live in Paris."

"Wow. Paris. Congratulations! When are you getting married?"

"We're still figuring out the details. Sometime next year, I think." I dipped a biscuit into my tea and chewed softly. "How old is your son?"

"He just turned three. His name is Nikhil."

"He's wonderful." *What about his mother?* I was so curious that I could barely eat the words. I remember looking toward his hands His left hand was hidden behind the teacup, so I wasn't able to discern a wedding ring.

"Yes, he is."

"Do you remember the last time we played with Lego blocks?" I motioned toward you as my own memories started to return.

He shook his head, so I continued. "It was right after Dadu's funeral. We started to build a house and then you got bored, so we chased you around the house. The three of us—you, me, and our other cousin, Shweta—we terrorized everyone."

"I wish I could remember," he whispered. "That was probably one of the last times I was with my mom."

I looked away and my eyes danced around the room. "I'm sorry."

"It's okay." He placed his tea on the table. "Naina didi, I do have to ask, why did you come here? After all this time, how did you find me?"

I shrugged. "We lost track of you. We never knew where you were, but a couple of weeks ago, something happened. It reminded me of you, so I decided to try to find you again."

"Again?"

I tilted my head and gulped down some more tea. "What do you know about what happened after your mom left?"

Nitu shook his head. "Not very much because I was so young. It was hard. My dad tried to hide it from me, but I could tell things weren't going well. We didn't have any money, and he lost his job. We moved back to our old place in Bombay, but he couldn't make it work there either. So we moved again when he took a construction job at South City. I tried to get work, too, when I was old enough. I worked at a few different restaurants and things turned around for us slowly."

I nodded. "I don't know the whole story, either," I hesitated. "We didn't know where you were, or your mom either. I did overhear something once. Your dad called Sameer Mama to ask for help. They were going to take you in for a while, but they never heard from him again. They tried to look for you, but we only knew your nickname, and after a while, I guess they gave up."

Nitu frowned and looked away. I could see his chest moving up and down rapidly as he tried to slow his breathing. "How did you find me now?"

I hastily placed my teacup on the table and decided to be upfront with him. "I had some help. I found your mom."

His skin turned pale and he squeezed his eyes shut. When he spoke a moment later, his voice was shaky. "You know where my mother is?"

"I do. It took a little while, but yes, I found her."

"Where, h-how, how is she?"

She's married and has a new family. "She's okay. She's still a doctor and does medical relief work in East Africa."

"Does she even remember me?"

"Yes. Of course." I forced a half smile. "Of course she does."

His eyes glazed over. I could see that he was revisiting whatever memories he had of her. "Did she tell you why she left?" The words caught in his throat, and I reached out and clasped his hand.

"No, not really. I'm sorry." I had decided that if we found Nitu and he asked me that very question, I could only answer in one way. It wasn't my place to tell him because that was Mashi's story to tell. I couldn't explain all of Mashi's behaviors and actions, anyway, because I still didn't understand them, and hadn't yet forgiven her fully myself.

"Someday maybe I'll ask her myself," he murmured.

I turned my attention back to my tea. *Should I tell him that she wanted him to visit?*

"How did you find her?"

"A private investigator found her information for me. And then I went to Taisoun and showed up at her house."

Nitu let out a painful chuckle. "Like you did here?"

"Pretty much."

"Do you think she would see me?"

I cocked my head to the side. "Yes, I feel certain she would." I raised my eyebrows as the full understanding of his question struck me. "Are you thinking of—?"

"No, no, of course not," he sighed. "I'm sorry. You came all this way to find me, and I've dredged up the past. The only thing that I've asked you about is my mother. You know, I thought I let the whole thing go, but I guess I was wrong."

"It's okay. Don't apologize. What happened in the past upended your life, I'm sure, and you were just a little kid. I understand. I wish I didn't have to reopen an old wound by coming to see you. But I'd like to get to know you, and your son, if you're willing."

Nitu beamed. "Nikhil, stop bugging your *Pishi's* friend and come over here," he called out to you.

"Hi, Nikhil," I said as you ran to us. "What were you doing over there?" I asked in Bengali.

"Building a space station," you answered, jumping up onto Nitu's lap.

"Nikhil, this is my cousin, my cousin-sister," Nitu said. "Naina didi came here to visit us."

"Want to see my Legos?" You were so sweet and lovable that my heart just melted.

"Yes, please." You grabbed my hand and dragged me to the pile of plastic blocks in the hallway. We spent the next hour building your space station on top of the yellow toy truck.

****

The next several days passed slowly. Getting to know Nitu was more laborious than I had anticipated. Twenty years was such a huge gap to bridge. Some relationships are easy enough to restart, but we were struggling. It wasn't that we disliked each other—far from it. We just had no common ground. He could barely remember our last meeting, and I only had a marginal recollection of it. We didn't know what to talk about. I felt bad describing my life. He'd grown up with so much less, and I didn't want to rub that in his face. I especially didn't want to talk about Dev's family because the differences in wealth and social class would be so vast. I still wasn't sure how much to tell him about my parents. Would it be a sore subject for him if I brought up my mom?

I also didn't know how to talk to him about Mashi. After that first conversation, he'd steered clear of the subject. Should I tell him about what she'd said during our visit? Her desire to see him, the reason she left, her new life with Tareq. It was all hers to tell and part of me wanted to keep it that way. Half of the time, I felt as if I owed Nitu the truth, but I didn't want to sully our chance at a relationship with details of Mashi's new life or half-baked reasons for why she abandoned him. I just didn't know where to start. How much of my trip to East Africa was fair game for us to talk about, and how much should I keep hidden? I also resisted asking him questions about her—to gather whatever details he remembered. I was interested in how much the woman who had left resembled the one that I had met in East Africa, but I kept my curiosity to myself.

When I wanted to ask about his life, I thought twice. How sensitive would he be about your biological mother? I didn't want to step on a land mine by asking where she was. At first, I suspected that the woman who had greeted me at the door that first day was your mom, but I quickly realized that she was only Nitu's housekeeper who helped look after you when he was at work. With all of those subjects to avoid, we didn't know where to begin. I was tempted to ask the PI to continue his investigation; a complete file would have provided me with any information I desired on his life, but I knew it wasn't my place. Once the address the PI had provided led to Nitu, I'd asked him to stop his investigation, so I actually never read the full file.

We found our common ground by spending time with you. Nitu would bring you over to the South City apartment, and I sat with you and your Lego blocks, puzzles, and movies for much of the day. At the time, he was working at a Chinese restaurant in New Alipur. Sometimes I would participate in your building projects; other times I would focus on my computer screen while keeping an eye on you with my peripheral vision. As I started to get to know you and Nitu better, my deadline grew closer and closer. I was supposed to return to Paris in the next two weeks, and I still hadn't been able to tell anyone in my family that I'd found Nitu. Another week passed by before I talked myself into bringing it up.

"Nitu, there's something I have to talk to you about." It was late, so the two of you were staying over, and we'd just put you to bed in the corner bedroom of the apartment, which also doubled as my dad's art studio after he'd taken up painting. After the first night that you spent there, it was really your room as much as it was his.

"Of course." He took a seat across from me on the couch and winced.

"Are you feeling okay?" I asked with a frown.

"It's nothing. I hurt my back a couple of years ago when I was working at a different restaurant. I tried to lift this heavy crate by myself. I should've asked for help, but I wanted to impress my boss. I must have wrenched it the wrong way tonight when I was lifting Nikhil out of the bathtub. It's happened before. I'll just take some aspirin before bed." He coughed as he rubbed the small of his back. "Anyway, what did you want to ask me about?"

I wrestled with the words, unsure of how to phrase my question. "Do you want to meet the rest of the family? Right now, they don't know that I found you, but I want to tell them." I held up my hand to stop him from interrupting me. "Before you say anything, I'm sure they would want to meet you."

A look of amusement passed across his face. "Thanks for talking to me about this, Naina didi. You don't need to be so worried. I'd love to meet them, especially any relatives here in Calcutta. With my dad gone, Nikhil needs more family." He turned his gaze toward the window, and I wondered where his mind had gone. I had refrained from asking so many questions, but he'd just opened the door a crack. I could walk through it if I wanted to do so. It was the only way past the awkwardness of avoided conversation topics.

So I did, or at least I started to. "What's on your mind?" I probed in a quiet voice.

"Just everything. It's so crazy that you're here now. I never expected to see any of you again."

I nodded. I wanted him to keep talking, and luckily enough, he did.

"Naina didi, I want us to be a family again." He glanced at the living room floor where you had begun to build your own version of the South City Complex with bright, multicolored Legos. The look on his face was a combination of hope and pain. "I want my son to have a different kind of home than the one I grew up in."

Before I could stop myself, the words were out. "What was it like for you? Growing up?"

He coughed again and shrugged. "I don't know. It was the way it was. After Ma left, Baba would tell me that she was just away on a long trip for work, helping people far away from home. That she would be back soon. But *soon* never came, and then I started to notice that her stuff was gone. I was six when she left, so I remembered some of their fights. They thought I didn't notice, but it's hard not to hear two people yelling at each other. At first, I was glad when there was no more yelling, but as I got older, I realized how empty everything was. Baba was always worried about paying the bills, so some days I stayed home from school to sell things on the street. I set up my own *luchi* stand on the weekends." He smirked. "I should make some for you sometime. I'm actually quite good at it."

"You might regret that offer."

"I think I'll be okay," he said with a wink.

"Do you remember her?"

He looked at me with wide eyes. "Ma? Yeah, I remember different things. Moments, feelings. I only wish that I understood why she left."

It wasn't really about you. I considered saying it, but I held back. *It's not my place to tell him.* I made a decision that I would never lie to him. I would evade some of his questions and leave out some of the details to spare his emotions and protect him, but never outright lie. Part of me also wanted to keep some of what had happened in East Africa as *my* memory—*my* moments with my aunt. Not everything was meant to be shared.

"Did she say anything to you?" he asked as if he could read my mind.

"She said a few things. I'm sure she would have said a lot more to you." My eyes narrowed slightly. "Do you want her phone number? It would probably be, well, probably be better if you talked to her yourself. She needs to be the one to explain because only she knows everything about that time."

"You're right. Soon, but not yet."

I nodded. "Can I take you to see Shweta tomorrow? Her parents—Sameer Mama and Ana *Mammie*—moved to Bombay last year, but she's still here a lot. I haven't said anything about you yet, but I know she would love to see you."

He picked up the glass of whiskey that he'd been nursing all evening and drained it in its entirety. As he put the glass back down on the end table, he glanced at his watch. "It's only eight o'clock. What if we went to see her now?"

I raised my eyebrows and looked at the clock in the hallway to confirm the time. "Sure. Let's do that."

We loaded your fast asleep form into the car and drove to your Shweta Mashi's place. I rang the doorbell and she opened the door, squealing in excitement when she saw me. She enveloped me into a huge hug, and when she finally released me, she peered past me at Nitu. "Is this Dev?" she asked. "You look different than in the pictures."

Nitu beamed and shook his head. "No, actually, I'm not Dev. Do you have any other guesses, Shweta didi?"

Shweta examined him closely, tilting her head from side to side. "You look so familiar. If I didn't know better…but, but it can't be."

"Maybe it can," I muttered.

A tiny spark lit in the center of her face and spread. "Nitu?"

He and I both nodded. Without waiting for any other acknowledgment, she jumped on him with the same kind of hug that she'd given me. When she released him, she pinched both of his cheeks.

She looked back and forth between Nitu and me. "How? When? I need to hear everything." She started to pull us into her living room, but Nitu dashed back to the car for you. Shweta's eyes grew large when he returned to the entryway with you in his arms, still sound asleep. She smiled when she saw your sweet face. "Is this darling boy yours, Nitu?" she asked as she shut the door behind us.

He nodded and smiled broadly, always the proud father.

"He's beautiful. I want to hear all about him too. Oh, this conversation is going to require tea and biscuits. I'll put some water on and be right back, but you're welcome to some of those sweets for now." She gestured at the dining table.

Nitu laid you down on a loveseat in the corner, and we sat on a larger sofa to wait for her to return from the kitchen. Even with all of the commotion around, you never stirred. You always could sleep through anything, Nikhil.

The rest of the night flew by. Shweta's presence made me feel less self-conscious that something about my life would trigger Nitu's sensitivities. The formality of our situation fell away and the three of us reveled in the childhood memories that we could recall. We went from three strangers who shared a few memories to three cousins getting to know each other again.

You've seen it. Shweta is a born storyteller and always the life of the party. I have no recollection of what we talked about—no details. Just laughter and smiles. Nitu took you back to South City around midnight, and we made plans to get together the next day. All of us had planned to tell Shweta's parents about both of you the next day. I stayed at her place that night instead of leaving with him. We had some catching up of our own to do.

We stayed up until three as I recounted everything that had happened. The background check that started my search. My trip to East Africa. Meeting Mashi. Coming to Calcutta and that first address in the slums. And finally, finding Nitu…and you.

That night sleep came easily—another weight had been lifted.

****

As soon as Shweta told her parents about Nitu, they dropped everything and flew to Calcutta for a visit. When we introduced Nitu to them, his interaction with them flowed more easily than it had with me. Perhaps they were less worried about upsetting him and just wanted to get to know him. Perhaps they had more in common with him since they had all grown up in India. I still don't know the real reason. Whatever it was, it was obvious from the get-go.

Questions cluttered my mind. I wanted to ask him so many things, but I was too scared to bring them up. I think he also knew that I hadn't shared everything about my trip to East Africa. With so many elephants in the room, our conversations remained structured and forced.

Things with you were different. I like to think that you fell in love with me on the first day we met. While that may not be true, you did warm to me very quickly. When you met the rest of the family, you were shy and huddled in the corner. You wouldn't stray far from either Nitu or me. The transition happened slowly. I was amazed to watch it firsthand. On the first day, all of the excitement and people overwhelmed you. By the end of the week, you were content to move from one person to the next. You had this uncanny ability to seek out and attain the maximum amount of *patha* from all of us. And we loved giving you the attention that you sought.

After spending so much time with you and Nitu, I found it hard to leave Calcutta. By that time, I'd been away almost two months. I missed Dev and I wanted to return to France, but I was drawn to the ambiance around me. There was so much joy in our everyday interactions that I was afraid to blink. You and Nitu had appeared so suddenly in my life. If I looked away, you might disappear. Would I ever find you again? I extended my departure a number of times, but finally could prolong my visit no further.

My eyes grew wet on the way to the airport and remained that way all through the flight. When I arrived at Charles De Gaulle Airport, Dev wrapped his arms around me. It was the end of my adventure and time to return to normal life.

It turns out that it was just the beginning.

****

May, 2017 – Things change in East Africa

I'm not sure when the rest of the world realized what was happening in Taisoun. One day the news cited a minor story about a protest at Taisoun University. I only happened upon it when I was browsing articles on Al-Jazeera. It didn't seem important enough to make any of the other major news sites. Within a day or two, the protest had disappeared from the news altogether, only to reappear a week later.

It started as just another Friday morning. After I woke up, I turned on the TV and flipped to BBC to catch the hourly news when I was greeted by a breaking news update. A series of images flashed across the screen. *Gunfire at Taisoun University. Upturned cars outside of campus. People running away from everything and toward nothing. Bodies lying in the streets.*

The initial protest at Taisoun University began when the commencement speaker, a Tunisian politician who was instrumental in the construction of the new government after the revolution, was denied entry into the city. The cover was a customs scam of some sort, but no one believed that he would have been stupid enough to try to smuggle alcohol into East Africa. Students shouted in the streets and then went silent.

The news didn't report why until that Friday morning.

After the first day of protests, the military entered the university's campus and fired shots into the air. They occupied the campus, lying in wait to quell any further threads of dissent. On Thursday night, a student snuck past the convoy and set fire to a statue of Bahtez, the East African president. The bronze statue was doused in gasoline and lit up. It remained standing but emerged scarred with scorch marks.

After that, the threads appeared again, but this time all over Taisoun, coordinated by social media and cell phone coverage. The military marched into two different neighborhoods, but were unable to contain it when the flood began. Citizens took to the streets in droves. Their chants echoed across the city. *"Down with Bahtez. Down with tyranny."*

I watched the chants that Friday morning in awe. Part of me wanted to rejoice at the potential triumph against a dictator. Bahtez had taken power in a military coup, and the East African people deserved better than his oppressive regime. But the other part of me knew better. Revolution is anything but clear-cut. It can have far-reaching consequences that are difficult to predict, and ousting a dictator does not necessarily mean that someone better will take over. Many people would die, even if the revolution were successful.

I gaped at the television, frozen in place. Dev woke up twenty minutes later and joined me on the couch, but I barely reacted when he put his arm around me. We watched the protest scenes replay as the university went up in flames. We still hadn't said a word to each other. He reached for the phone and handed it to me.

My fingers shook as I dialed Mashi's number. The first time that I tried, the call wouldn't even connect. I tried again and the phone rang four times before Mashi picked up. Static enveloped our voices, so I could barely hear her.

"Mashi? It's Naina."

"Hi, *betu*. How are you?"

I exhaled rapidly. "I'm fine," I yelled into the phone. "Tell me about you. We're watching the news right now."

"Don't worry, betu," she said through the crackling. "Everything will calm down in a couple of days."

"But the news, it says—"

"Naina, the news is always dramatic. We're fine."

"Okay, but just stay at home. Don't go into Taisoun," I urged.

"Don't be silly. I'm not planning to go into Taisoun, but I can't stay home. I have to go to work at the hospital. They've called in all of the doctors."

"Of course. Because so many people are wounded. I just want you to take care of yourself. Please be safe."

The line cleared up momentarily, and I heard her sigh. "I'll take care, don't worry. Everything's going to be fine." The static returned before she could finish the sentence.

I took a deep breath and decided that I didn't want to pick a fight. "Okay, okay."

"I have to go. Just remember that the news always makes things look worse than they really are. I'll talk to you soon, okay?"

"Bye, Mashi," I said as the line clicked.

Later that morning, Dev and I both went to work. We agreed that Mashi was right—the news does often make situations sound more dramatic than they actually are. Still, I couldn't shake the images that I'd seen.

****

The next two weeks passed by like a blur. The memories are hazy. I guess my mind blocked them out. A few days turned a one-off protest in Taisoun into the East African revolution.

Every day we woke up to the news of further and continuing protests. More people seemed to be joining the fight. The media began to report death estimates. First, eight people were killed in clashes with the army. Then another fifteen. Then twenty-two. For each death on the streets, ten more people enlisted in the protests. At my office, I watched the buzz on Facebook and Twitter instead of attending to conference calls and financial reports. People around me were doing the same as they compared it to what happened in Egypt and Tunisia in 2011. I remained quiet as their conversations droned on in the background. This time, it was different for me. This time, I had a personal stake.

I spoke to Mashi in the mornings. Occasionally, I could get through on the phone, but other times we had to rely on chat services. Again and again, I tried to convince her to visit us in Paris, or even Nitu in India. She remained adamant about staying in East Africa. Her husband was a government employee and he was secretly providing the rebels with small-scale supplies that he was able to procure. While he dared not officially join the protests, the thought of leaving amounted to desertion for him, and Mashi refused to consider leaving without him. I compelled her to convince him, to reason with him. What good could he do the revolution if he were dead?

****

"Mashi, I need you to tell me the truth. How bad is it now?"

I could tell she was contemplating how much to tell me. Too much truth would send us into a panic, but too little and I would never believe her. Finally, she answered, "It's getting bad now. The hospitals are full. I lost a couple of patients. But the protesters are gaining ground. It will all be over soon."

"Why can't you take a vacation? You can always go back in a few weeks if things have calmed down. Is this really worth risking your life over?"

"Come on, Naina. If this were happening in your city, would you want to leave?"

Yes, actually, I would. I was tempted to say so, but I restrained myself. Our situations were anything but comparable. I grew up surrounded by such a range of cultures. While I love many of the cities I've lived in, no single one stands out the way Taisoun seemed to for Mashi. You've seen this in my arguments with your father. Moving is much easier for me to contemplate because I still don't feel as if I belong to any one country, let alone any particular city. I don't know when Taisoun became that for Mashi, but I pushed myself to understand. "I don't want anything to happen to you. We need more time. I want to get to know you. Maybe I'm being selfish, but I don't care."

Asking her to take care of herself is not selfish, I reminded myself as my thoughts shifted to Nitu. I'd received several e-mails from him. He'd asked for updates on the situation in East Africa and if I'd heard from Mashi. I was ducking many of his messages and being vague when I did respond. I didn't know what to tell him. I had no idea how he would react. If only I had, well, things would probably be very different.

"*Aray,* betu, stop worrying," she scolded. "This will all just be a blip in our memories after a few months."

"But look at what happened in Egypt. It took four years to get things under control after the revolution, and Syria's still a mess. Do you really think Bahtez will give up power that easily?"

"I have faith in this movement."

"But why do you need to stay there right now? Let things calm down, then go back and help them rebuild. You don't need to be there right now." *You can't help if you're dead. This movement isn't enough to set up a new government.* I wanted so much to say it, but I refrained. It would have been pointless. I wouldn't be able to convince her, and I risked creating more distance between us. We certainly couldn't afford that with all of the other sources of tension.

"Naina, my place is here. Tareq needs to stay here, and I'm not leaving without him."

"Why must he come before the rest of your family? What about the rest of us? We're here too, and we were your family long before he came into the picture." The words escaped from my mouth before I could stop them. I was left with my mouth open, wide-eyed and looking at the phone. *Don't hang up on me,* I mentally pleaded. *We've come this far.*

The line remained silent for several painful moments. "I'm sorry for what happened in the past," Mashi said in a restrained voice that I could hear clearly even with the shakiness of the line. "But I can't do anything to change that."

"Okay," I acceded. I was so relieved that she hadn't hung up that I could no longer protest anything. My heart was racing, and although I didn't say anything to her, I began looking for news articles on my tablet about the 2011 Egyptian revolution. A list of headlines appeared, which I quickly scanned. My lungs tightened further and I stifled a gasp.

"Let's talk about something else," Mashi tried to change the subject in a forced tone. We both knew that we had come a long way, and it wasn't worth retreating because of one outburst. "How is your work going? Do you have any more trips to Africa planned?"

"Not for another couple of months," I said quietly. When Dev and I last discussed my travel schedule, I had mentioned making another stop in Taisoun. That seemed more like a bad idea with each passing day. "I have a trip to India planned for work in two weeks, so I'll make a stop in Calcutta as well."

"What projects are you working on now?"

"I have a few different ones. A small assignment in Delhi. One in Mozambique and one in Lesotho. Maybe one more in Uganda."

"It all sounds so exciting," Mashi said brightly.

I pursed my lips. "It isn't nearly as glamorous as everyone seems to think, but I enjoy it overall."

"Good, good."

Silence overtook us once again, and I debated whether I should bring up Nitu. I finally decided to go for it. The conversation was dead in the water anyway, and I had yet to tell her that I had found him. I hadn't even had the chance to tell her about you. I had no idea how she would take such news, but I knew that if we were to have any kind of real relationship that I had to start being honest.

"Mashi, there's something else that we need to talk about."

"Of course, betu. What is it? Please don't worry about me here. Everything will be fine. We aren't leaving, but we aren't being reckless either."

I could tell she was pretending to have no idea what topic I was about to broach. The apprehension in my voice must have made it obvious that we were going to talk about one of two things: either I had told my mom about my trip in all its glorious detail and was communicating her reaction, or I was going to talk about what had happened with Nitu. I still hadn't mentioned the East African portion of my trip to either of my parents, just the Indian one. My mother was looking forward to meeting Nitu when she returned to India, and I'd even connected the two of them on Skype earlier that morning.

"I never told you what happened after I left Taisoun."

"Yes?" Mashi's voice trembled.

I swallowed, but the words lingered on the tip of my tongue.

"Yes, betu? Tell me."

"I found him. I found Nitu." I steadied myself by placing my left hand on my knee and grasping tightly. After a deep breath, I leaned back into the couch with the phone in my other hand.

She exhaled rapidly. "You did?"

"Yes. I did."

She responded with a flood of questions. "What did he say? How is he? What is he like? Is he married? Tell me everything. Please."

"I, well, we're still getting to know each other. He seems happy in general." I struggled with whether or not to mention you. "He, er, isn't married…at the moment," I continued, postponing discussion on your absent mother.

"Can you send me a picture of him?"

"Of course." I breathed a sigh of relief. She hadn't asked me any of the questions that I would have absolutely no idea how to answer. *Is he still angry with me? Do you think he would want to see me? Did you tell him about how you found him? Did you meet anyone else in his family?* I'm not sure why, but I wasn't ready to tell her about you. How would she react if she knew that she had a grandchild as well? How did I want her to react? Would Nitu be comfortable with her knowing about you? Those questions drew blanks in my mind, so I didn't want to venture near them. "I'll send you the picture later today."

"Thank you, Naina. I have to get to work now, but thank you."

"Mashi, wait. There's more."

"Yes?"

"I told him that I had met you, and that you're in East Africa."

"*Achha?*" The surprise in her voice was clear.

"He called me this morning because he's worried about you too. He hasn't confirmed it, but I think he might want to meet you sometime soon."

"Really?" Her voice cracked.

"Yes, Mashi."

"Do you think it would be okay if I wrote to him?"

My face broke out into a smile. "Send me a letter. I'll give it to him on my trip."

****

May, 2017 – From bad to worse

During the next two weeks, the world watched the situation in East Africa worsen steadily. President Bahtez appeared on television a number of times. He condemned the protests and accused the protesters of treason. Despite their efforts, he remained adamant and refused to step down. The crowds in the streets grew larger, even as some were beaten, trampled, and killed.

The first time I heard about the presidential guard firing tear gas into the crowds, I felt dazed. The reaction was expected with everything that I had read about the Arab Spring, but with Mashi so close by, I struggled to bear it. After I heard it a few times, though, it became routine commentary. My only comfort was my conversations with Faisal. He'd remained on the ground there, and I knew that he would be honest with me about the situation. As a UN employee, he would be evacuated as soon as the situation became too tense for the organization to stomach. So far, that hadn't happened, and I clung to that piece of hope. Neither he nor I understood why it hadn't happened, but he was happy that he could stay with Arya. Speaking to him reassured me. Perhaps the situation really wasn't as bad as the news portrayed?

My assignment in Delhi was particularly hellish, and when I reached Calcutta afterward, I was exhausted and brain dead. Shweta picked me up from the airport, and when we reached the South City apartment, there was a surprise waiting for me. Nitu was already sitting in the living room, and you were there with him. I remember walking into the apartment to see the two of you practically submerged in a tub of ice cream. The sight was so comforting that I dropped my bag by the door and joined you for the treat.

We watched *The Jungle Book* that night, which later became one of your favorite childhood movies. I'm sure you'll be reacquainted with it in a few years when your own baby is old enough to watch it.

In all of these years, I can only think of a handful of times when I've seen you looking quite that happy. Watching one of your favorite movies with a tub of ice cream in your lap. Pure contentment.

After the movie, we put you to bed, and the three of us continued gossiping in the living room. It was wonderful to feel as if I had siblings for those small snippets of my memory. I'm sure you understand what I mean. You would probably be a very different person without your sister. As an only child, the time I spent with my cousins was even more precious.

A couple of hours later, Shweta passed out next to you in one of the bedrooms while Nitu and I stayed in the living room. I felt jetlagged and wired. He looked exhausted, but he humored me by staying up. With Shweta gone, the walls of formality between us were back up, albeit slightly lower than they once were. There were still questions that I wanted to ask, things that I wanted to say, but I had no idea how. We were discussing one of my projects when I remembered the letter from Mashi.

"Hold on a second," I said standing up. "There's something that I have to give you, before I forget." *Or decide that it's a bad idea.* I opened my suitcase and retrieved the letter from the top compartment after rifling through old receipts and other documents. As she'd requested, I'd printed the scanned copy of her handwritten note. Since I'd promised not to read it, Dev was actually the one who printed it and sealed it in an envelope. It took a lot of restraint not to open it, but I'd successfully resisted.

"Mashi and I've spoken a few times since I left East Africa. She wanted me to give this to you when she heard I was coming back to Calcutta." I handed Nitu the letter. "I didn't read it. Dev printed it out and sealed it in the envelope for me."

He handled the letter gingerly from the corner, as if he didn't want to touch it. "Do you want me to open it here?" he asked.

"That's up to you. Like I said, I didn't read it. If you want me to be here when you open it, then I will be. But if you want some privacy, then take it home, or I can go lie down in my room. We can talk about it later, if that's what you want, or we can never mention it again," I shrugged. "Whatever you prefer."

Nitu drew a deep long breath. "I'll open it here."

"Are you sure?" I reiterated.

He stared at the letter for a moment and nodded. "You actually get to be my didi now. I want you to stay while I," he hesitated, "while I read a letter from the first woman who abandoned me."

I inhaled sharply. I wanted to ask what he meant, but I remained silent. *Who was the second?* I glanced at the bedroom where you were sleeping, and then I understood. I slid over to him and gave him a hug.

"Nitu, I'm going to make you some chamomile tea. You can open it whenever you're ready."

"Okay."

A few minutes later, I returned with two steaming-hot teacups. I placed them on the table and waited patiently. Once I was seated, he eased his finger under the edge to break the envelope's seal. The way he did it reminded me of the way my parents open presents—Dad in particular. Your Nannu makes sure that every bit of the wrapping paper can be reused. *Nitu fits right in with the family.*

The seal finally gave way and he inched the letter out. He unfolded it and passed it to me.

I frowned. "Aren't you going to read it?"

"I want you to read it to me."

"No." I shook my head. "If you really want me to read it, I'll look at it after you do. But this letter is for you, and that means you have to be the first person to read it."

He bit his lip, but accepted the letter as I gave it back to him. His posture was rigid as he read it. When he was done, he placed the letter on the table. "Read it."

"Are you sure?"

"Yeah." Nitu retreated into the bedroom where you were sleeping as I picked up the letter.

My dear Nitu,

I don't know where to begin. There is no explanation for how much of your life I have missed over the years. I've thought of you so often, but I haven't had the courage to seek you out. I was so scared that you would never want to see me again that I just let the days pass. I kept saying I would try tomorrow and then the next day, and time just slipped away from me.

When Naina told me that you had asked about me, I realized how many opportunities I let disappear. You are my son, and while I cannot turn back the clock, I would very much like to get to know you. East Africa is hardly the ideal destination at the moment, but as soon as things calm down, I would be elated if you would come for a visit. I haven't been back to India since I left, but I would return to Calcutta to visit you, if that's what you prefer instead.

If you agree, then please ask Naina to give you my contact details. I do hope that I hear from you, but I understand if you would prefer not to respond.

With all of my love,

Ma

I wasn't sure what to do when I put the letter down. *She didn't really say much,* I remember thinking. *But what could she put in such a letter?* That was the big question. It was their first contact in two decades. I was glad that she hadn't used the letter to try to explain all of the time that had passed or why she had left. Her words were simple. *Leave the past in the past and try to rebuild in the present.* She wanted to get to know her son now, before it was too late for her. All she had to do was ask him if he felt the same way.

Nitu reappeared on the couch next to me, and we drank our tea without acknowledging the letter. I turned on the TV, and the second *Dhoom* movie droned on in the background. We watched it for about an hour in silence. The only sound that escaped me was a giggle at how short Aishwarya Rai's skirt was in her first song. I don't remember much else.

When the credits started to roll, I turned off the TV. "Penny for your thoughts?" I asked.

Nitu gave me a puzzled look. "What does that mean?"

"It's just an old saying. It means that I would give you a penny to tell me what you're thinking about."

"That isn't very much."

I tossed a cushion at him and waited.

"I don't know, didi. I don't know what to say or think."

"How do you feel?"

"Numb. She's been out of my life for so long. And then you showed up and everything started to turn topsy-turvy."

I beamed at his reference to Enid Blyton. "Did you know that I was reading Enid Blyton the first time we met? When we were all here for Dadu's funeral."

"Yeah, I do." Nitu glanced at the ceiling. "That's how my mom convinced me to read her books. She said, 'Your didi was reading this, don't you want to read it too?' For some reason, I do remember that vividly."

I blinked rapidly and felt a smile spread across my face. I was so touched by what he'd said. *He started to read Enid Blyton because I did.* I suppressed some of my reaction because I didn't want to overwhelm him. What would the appropriate response be? I didn't want to be overly affectionate. We were still getting to know each other. "So topsy-turvy…big sisters will do that, huh?"

"Don't worry, you're not the only woman in my life to turn everything upside down." He kept his eyes fixed on the ceiling.

I rubbed my hands together for a moment. "Tell me more." Nitu had given me an opening to learn more about him, and I wasn't going to miss the opportunity.

"There's not much to tell. Women come into my life, and before I even notice or realize it, they've changed each and every little thing."

"That's not necessarily a bad thing." There was pain in his expression, though, so I asked what was really on his mind. "Are you still talking about me? Or someone else?"

The question fluttered to the ground like a feather before he answered. "How perceptive of you…" He drank the final bit of his tea. "I think you already know the answer to that question."

I considered pushing him to say more, but he only held my gaze for a moment. Immediately, I knew that our secrets had just rebuilt the walls between us. Each day we spent together, we chipped away at them. The walls came down and were reconstructed, each time a bit lower than the previous day. But for that night, there was nothing left to be said.

"I'm going to turn in. See you in the morning," Nitu said as he stood up.

"Sleep well."

****

The next morning Nitu came into my room and shook me awake. I was grumpy and groggy as I sat up in bed.

"It's so earlyyyy. Why don't you go back to bed?" I slid down onto my pillow and turned over on to my stomach.

"I couldn't sleep."

"I'm sure you can get a couple of hours in." I pulled the covers up to my face to block out the light.

"Naina didi, wake up. I need to talk to you."

I groaned and peeked at him from the corner of the blanket.

"Have you seen the news this morning?"

"Nitu, I'm not even awake yet. No, I haven't seen the news. Let me sleep." The fog of jet lag remained motionless above my head. "I'll watch the news in a few hours."

He plonked down on the bed and grabbed my tablet from the bedside table. "Look at the news."

"If I watch whatever you have to show me, will you let me go back to sleep?"

"Sure."

I shot him a glare and fumbled through my passcode to unlock the tablet. By the time he tapped through to open a news app, my eyes were glazing over again.

He nudged me, and I sighed. "Well, come on then, let's see it."

The BBC report yanked me awake. *Scenes of Horror in Taisoun* appeared across the bottom of the screen as the news anchor spoke.

> *"The following report contains some graphic images.*
>
> *Last night, protesters overtook Khalifa Street outside of the Presidential Palace and chanted for the resignation of East African President Omar El-Bahtez into the early morning. At four thirty this morning, police forces descended upon the crowds with tear gas and concussion grenades. A number of demonstrators were beaten by plainclothes officers, and several police cars were set on fire. When the frantic crowds began to push back rather than disperse, gunshots were heard. Police officials have said that officers did fire their weapons into the air to break up the crowds, but some witnesses are claiming officers fired into the crowds. A number of deaths have been reported, and it has yet to be determined if any of the protesters were*

shot. It is confirmed that seven men were beaten to death, and at least eight others are reported dead, but we do not yet know the causes of those deaths. Witnesses say that many who did escape were severely injured. The death toll is likely to rise as we receive further information about…"

"That's enough," I said as I exited the app. I didn't want to endure any more of the news report.

"She needs to leave East Africa. We need to get her to leave."

"What do you think I've been trying to do? She won't do it. Her husband wants to support the movement. They won't leave." *Oh shit.* I still hadn't told Nitu that Mashi had remarried.

"Husband?" Nitu looked at me like a wounded puppy that had been kicked in the gut. "She has a husband?" he repeated.

I took a deep breath with a long exhale. *Too late now.* The time for discretion had passed. "Yes. She remarried at some point. I don't know when."

"He's East African?"

"Yes."

"You didn't tell me about him." His tone was hurt and accusatory.

"I know. I'm sorry, Nitu. I didn't know what to say. I hoped she would tell you in the letter. I didn't know what to tell you myself and what I should let her tell you. Just like I haven't told her about Nikhil so that you could, if you ever even wanted to speak with her."

"Did you meet him? When you were there?"

"No. He was away on some business trip."

"I see. Does she have any other children? Another son?" Nitu stood up with a stony expression.

"No, Nitu. I promise. You are her only child." I looked directly into his eyes because I didn't want him to think I was keeping any other secrets about Mashi.

He nodded once and looked at the floor. "You should have told me about the husband."

"I know. I'm sorry."

Nitu was at the door before he glanced back at me and nonchalantly said, "I'm going to get her to leave East Africa."

****

May, 2017 – Nitu's decision

We spent most of the day tiptoeing on eggshells. Neither of us brought up the news about East Africa. I sent Faisal a message to find out what was happening. His reply didn't say much more than the news report, only that it had calmed down since the protest had started. Part of me wanted him to say that the UN was evacuating because it would have given me leverage to push Mashi to leave while she still could.

I ran some errands and went to see Mamta for a while. Nitu stayed in the apartment while I was gone. The two of you had taken up an interim residence in the South City apartment, and I was glad that someone was making use of it.

When I returned to the apartment, the lights were already out. I crept to my room and got ready for bed. It took me a while to fall asleep. The ceiling became more and more interesting as the minutes went by. I started to mentally map out all of the possibilities of what Nitu might be thinking. Would he dream about his mother's new family? Was he only focused on getting her to leave East Africa? How did he plan to accomplish that? I'd been trying to convince her for weeks. If she heard it from her son, though—maybe? Could he be more persuasive?

I'm not sure how long I lay there with my eyes wide open. My body wanted nothing more than sleep, but my mind was running at full speed. I was about to give up and reach for the book I had been reading when I saw a crack of light seep in under the door from the living room. *Nitu's awake?* I dragged myself out of bed.

He was engrossed in my computer's screen when he heard me approach. "Hi," he said.

I noticed an article about flights to Taisoun on the screen. "Talk to me." My tone was more forceful than I intended, but alarm bells were going off in my head. *Why was he looking at flights to Taisoun?*

Nitu didn't even look up. "I'm going to visit her."

"That, that's great. Hopefully things will calm down soon enough for you to go." We both knew that wasn't what he meant, but I clung desperately to my wishful thinking.

"Maybe they will. I hope so." He shrugged. "But I'm not going to wait to find out."

"But—"

"Don't even try to stop me, Naina didi. We'll just fight, and I don't want that," Nitu interrupted.

I opened my mouth and closed it again. "I don't want to fight either, but this doesn't make sense. Why now? After all this time? Why not just wait?"

He took a gulp of something that looked suspiciously like whiskey. It was too far away for me to smell it, so I didn't know for sure. "I don't know. I feel like if I wait, I'll never get this chance. Isn't that what she said? She kept putting it off, and one day led to one more day. I'm not going to make that mistake."

I joined him at the dining room table. Once I was closer, I could smell the intensity of the whiskey. I pushed his glass aside and looked him in the eyes. "What chance?"

"What do you mean 'what chance'? The chance to see her again. If things get worse there…What if something happens to her? I would never be able to forgive myself."

"Okay. I know you're worried. I am too. But what about your safety? Isn't that important too? Mashi knows East Africa much better than you do. If she thinks things are fine, she's probably right. What if something happened to you?" My eyes wandered toward your bedroom door. "What about Nikhil? If something happens to you, what then? I don't see his mother helping out around here."

Nitu recoiled at what I'd said. "I want to be able to tell my son that while he may not have a mother, he does have a grandmother."

"What happened with her, Nitu? Where is she?"

He downed the remainder of his whiskey. "Most people in my life can't wait to leave."

I reached for his hand. "Come on. Shweta and I are here, aren't we?"

"Sure, for now. But soon you'll be married and living with that fancy family. It'll be the same for her. You'll disappear just as they always do. My mom wants to get to know me now. She wants me back, and I can't miss out on this chance."

I felt as if he'd just skewered me with a kitchen knife. "That's not fair. I don't live here, but I'm not going to disappear on you just because I'm marrying into a wealthy family."

He sighed. "I'm sorry. I'm just upset."

I helped myself to a glass of water from the pitcher on the table, unable to meet his eyes. Nitu had apologized, but I could tell that he had meant what he said, that he believed it.

"Naina didi, I'm scared. What if something happens to her before I get to meet her? I could lose this chance. I have to go."

I threw my hands out to the sides. "A couple of days ago you weren't even sure if you wanted to get to know her. Now you're risking everything to meet her? She sends a letter so you're going to risk your life to go to her?"

"If I decide that I don't want her to be a part of my life, I want it to be my decision. Not because of some revolution in the dessert."

"What about Nikhil? Who's going to take care of him? Can we take him to his mother's?" It was a long shot, but I threw diplomacy to the winds. "Tell me about her. Please, I want to know about Nikhil's mother."

A faraway look passed across his face. "She was wonderful. And then she left."

I wanted to ask him more, although I sensed that he wasn't going to tell me. I still made a final effort. "That's it? What happened?"

"I don't know. One day she just left."

"I'm sorry, Nitu." I squeezed his hand.

He groped under the table and retrieved a familiar bottle of whiskey. "You must think I'm crazy. Now I'm going to open the door for another woman, one who already abandoned me."

He was about to dole out another large helping of whiskey into his glass when I grabbed the glass and pulled it out of reach. "I think you've had enough." For good measure, I reclaimed the bottle as well. *Glenlivet Archive 21,* I read on the label. "Where did you get this?"

"One of the cabinets in the kitchen."

"My dad kept this for a special occasion. You shouldn't have taken it."

Nitu made a goofy expression. I could tell he'd already had far too much.

I gritted my teeth and returned the bottle to the kitchen. When I emerged, I took a seat across from him again. "Are you sure about this?"

"About going to East Africa?"

I nodded.

"I'm sure." Nitu was drunk, but I could still sense the plea in his expression. "Will you come with me?"

Part of me was touched. Did he really want me to be with him for such a pivotal moment of his life? My immediate instinct was to say yes, but when I opened my mouth to speak, reason prevailed. "No. I couldn't go there now. Even if the situation there were different, I'm not ready to see her again. Besides, Dev would never let me go back now. But I'll see if Faisal can help you with the visa and with protection once you're there."

"Naina didi, if anything happens to me—"

I raised my hands to stop him. "Let's not go there right now. Don't worry, I'll make sure that you're taken care of. Just don't do anything stupid, okay? At least not any stupider than going there in the first place."

****

There are so many things that I should have done differently that day. I gave up on convincing Nitu too easily. I still don't understand why I caved. I guess I wanted to believe him when he said everything would be okay. More than anything, I understood why he so desperately did not want to wait. What if he waited and something happened? What if he lost the chance to speak with Mashi because we decided it was more prudent to wait another couple of months? What if the situation in East Africa became even worse? Once the airports were closed, he would lose his ability to make that choice. Maybe if I hadn't already met her, I would have been motivated by the same logic.

****

When I asked Faisal for help with Nitu's visa, he reacted as if I'd gone certifiably insane. "Why on earth do you want me to help get someone from your family *into* East Africa?"

I kept things short and to the point. I didn't want to get into a massive discussion. Nitu had made his choice, so I kept to the crux of it. "He was going to try to get in no matter what, so I was hoping that you could make the process a bit smoother and safer."

Even with the crappy connection, I could tell that Faisal heard the insistence in my voice. He looked at me through the webcam view and squinted to get a read on my expression. "Who is this guy?"

"My cousin."

The connection delayed delivery of what I said, but as soon as he heard it, he raised his eyebrows. "You said that the aunt you came to see had a son, right? So this cousin, he's her son?"

"Yes, the son I told you she left in India. With everything happening in East Africa, Nitu doesn't want to wait. He's scared he will lose his chance to see his mother. Please, Faisal, I can't stop him from going," I pleaded.

Faisal crossed his arms and sighed. "Okay, I'll see what I can do. My supervisor is going to flip shits, but I should be able to make something work."

"Thank you."

"You owe me big time, but I'll accept one of those desserts that you used to make."

I grinned. "Tiramisu or fudge cake?"

"Actually, I need both for a favor this big."

"Done!" When the upbeat moment subsided, I turned serious again. "How are things there?"

"Really tense. I don't think we'll be evacuated unless things get much worse, but a lot of people think that will be soon."

"What about your girl?"

He straightened up in his seat. "I spoke to Arya's father. We decided to get married sometime next year."

My posture stiffened and I threw my hands out to the sides. "Dude, that's amazing. You just totally dropped that as if it was nothing?"

The corners of his mouth curled slightly. "I did, didn't I? Yeah, we're getting married."

"Congratulations."

"Thank you."

"Are they still in Taisoun?" I asked hesitantly.

Faisal shook his head. "I convinced them to take an early vacation, so they're in Addis at the moment. They wanted to be close, so I set it up with a friend in the office there."

"At least it's close enough that you can visit."

"Yeah."

My face broke out into a big smile. "I'm so excited for you. It's the year of commitments, isn't it?"

"I guess so." He looked away for a moment. "All right, Naina, I have to go. I'll work on that stuff for your cousin."

****

Faisal came through with his promise in less than a week. I sent him Nitu's passport information, which he submitted directly to the Ministry of Foreign Affairs. Two days later, he delivered a page that would confirm Nitu's visa, which would be provided officially at the airport upon his arrival. Because we were in such a rush, we used the visa-on-arrival procedure, rather than sending his passport to the embassy in India. I wasn't completely comfortable with the approach, but Nitu was adamant about the need for expediency.

Nitu and I called Mashi together to tell her that he would be coming. Her initial reaction was shock, followed shortly by elation, and then replaced by concern. I soothed her worries by explaining how Faisal was going to provide a UN escort. In the same conversation, I also tried to convince myself, to no avail.

After we explained to Shweta that we needed help to look after you, she called her parents, and they flew in from Bombay once again. We took you to their old flat where you would stay while Nitu was in East Africa. We explained that he would be away for a maximum of two weeks. We didn't give any of them much detail, not even Shweta, other than mentioning that he had to travel urgently. They didn't ask too many questions. You were so cute and lovable that they didn't even care why you would be spending that time with them. All of their attention was focused on your tiny little form bouncing around the apartment.

I wish they had asked. If we'd had to explain things, maybe they could have talked some sense into Nitu. I was the only one who knew where he was going and why. He probably only told me because he needed my help to arrange it, or perhaps it was because I was the only one who had been in contact with Mashi. Whatever the reason, he did tell me, and I did help him. I still wonder whether I did the right thing.

****

On the day Nitu arrived in Taisoun, Faisal sent me a message that he'd picked up Nitu at the airport and dropped him at Mashi's home in Om Tais. I called her that evening and chatted briefly with both of them. I could sense the uncertainty and awkwardness they were both feeling on the other end of the line, so I kept the call short. They would need time on their own to focus on each other, rather than dealing with me butting into the middle of it.

The first week after he arrived, things were eerily calm in Taisoun, but I was in a constant state of panic. I was sure that the other shoe would drop any second. Two nights in a row, I watched explosions go off in my dreams. When I awoke from the nightmares, I groped frantically for my tablet to check the news. The protests remained calm, but my mind could not accept it.

Much to Dev's chagrin, I extended my stay in Calcutta instead of going home to Paris. When I explained that it was to spend more time with you, he understood without any further discussion.

I know you don't remember it, but I think you actually absorbed much of what was happening. You knew that your Baba was away. We had explained as much. When you asked why, I told you that he had gone to find someone, and that the person was important to both of you. You asked when he would be back, and I said as soon as he could. The explanation made you somber, but you accepted it. You missed him so much, but you were still willing to enjoy the time with the rest of the family and me. You knew exactly how much mischief you could get away with. Your antics always came to a screeching halt just shy of crossing the line before you got into any real trouble. Well, back then anyway.

Those moments before the storm have always been precious to me.

****

June, 2017 – The storm

When Dev and I first saw the news report of that gruesome protest, I thought that the situation in East Africa couldn't possibly get any worse. People were already dying in the streets. What more could happen? Rationally, I could have come up with a few different scenarios. Things could devolve to mirror what happened in Afghanistan during the rise of the Taliban, or the situation could move past major protests in the streets. The military could begin attacking communities rather than trying to squash the uprisings. My mind created these and many more "worst-case" scenarios after Nitu left for East Africa. None of them prepared me for what would ensue in Taisoun.

The day started simply—a morning like any other after Nitu's departure. You were staying with me that night because Shweta's parents had gone to visit one of her father's properties a few hours north. After I pulled myself out of bed, I tiptoed into your room to check on you. Since you were still fast asleep, I took a quick shower, got dressed, and sat down at my computer.

About an hour later, I heard you stir. You'd been sleeping a lot—maybe it was a way to pass the time, or some kind of psychological reaction to your Baba being gone, I don't know. I sat with you for a moment and then set you up in front of the learning computer that Dev had suggested I get for you. It used games to teach you letters and numbers, and you'd been going through it at a breakneck pace. I've never seen a kid take so well to a toy that wasn't really a toy. You loved it. All I had to do to teach you was put you in front of it.

Since Nitu's departure, I'd taken to delaying my review of the news. I was too scared to look, so I didn't. That day was no exception.

I'd just left you with the learning computer when I heard my phone buzz. I remember the call taking me by surprise. *Who would call me this early in the morning?* Dev wouldn't be awake yet, and while the rest of my local family was most definitely up, they knew better than to phone me before nine. I rummaged through my purse and found it. The caller ID read "Shweta," which startled me even more. Shweta worked late nights managing her family's restaurant, and she was one of the few in our family who was fond of sleeping past ten. *Of all people, why is she calling me so early?* I answered before I could process the possibilities.

"Hey, Shweta. What's going on? Why are you up so early?"

"Have you heard from Nitu today?" Her voice sounded frantic.

"Er…no. I haven't been up very long. Is everything okay?" *What could have happened?*

I heard her take a deep breath. "Is Nikhil awake?"

"Yeah. He's at his little computer."

"You need to watch the news, but use headphones on your computer, or move him to his room." I could hear my heart thundering in my ears. There was only one reason she would want me to make sure that you couldn't hear the news.

"Okay. I'll, I'll call you back in a few minutes."

I grabbed my headphones and sat down with my iPad, careful to turn it around so that you could not see the screen. After plugging in my headphones, I opened the BBC app and turned on the live news feed.

> *"Early this morning, the situation in the East African capital Taisoun took a turn for the*

worst. Without warning, incumbent President Bahtez ordered his troops to raid three communities in parts of the city where a large number of protesters allegedly reside. We have limited information at the moment on the death toll, but what we see in the streets is that some faction of the military has broken away from following these orders. There is fighting everywhere. UN Secretary General Ban Ki Moon has called upon the government to halt these military actions. We'll now go to our local correspondent, Sheila King. Can you tell us what's happening on the ground, Sheila?"

The news control room split the screen to include a camera shot of a woman standing on the curb of a residential street in Om Tais. The station wagon parked on the street next to her was marred with smashed windows. Smoke poured from the doorway of a home across the street and from another home two blocks down from her, with a number of local residents attempting to put it out with simple garden hoses.

"Yes, James. At about five o'clock this morning, a military detail raided a relatively affluent community here in Om Tais, a wealthy suburb on the western side of Taisoun. About fifteen minutes later, two simultaneous raids were initiated in two residential communities in northern Taisoun. We have reports that shortly after, a group of militants showed up in the area where the two sides are now battling each other. It's not clear who these militants

are, but their insignia makes it likely that they are a rebel faction of the East African military that has defected in favor of the protesters."

"What kind of numbers do you see on both sides?"

"The military detail that raided this community in Om Tais was about fifty strong. As you can see behind me, the area has been badly damaged, and people are working to put out a number of fires. The detail entered at five and was gone about half an hour ago at six. We're still getting reports on the number of casualties, but so far I can confirm thirty dead and another fifty critically injured."

I'm not sure what either of them said after that. All I could do was stare at the community behind the reporter. *Om Tais*. The words echoed in my mind. Mashi lived in Om Tais. I did not recognize the buildings on the screen, but I had hardly explored her entire neighborhood. I reached for the phone and dialed her number.

"We are unable to connect your call," a recorded female voice said in a British accent. The voice then repeated the same in Arabic.

I hung up and tried the temporary phone that Nitu had picked up after he arrived in East Africa. The same recorded voice replied with an automated message.

The fear that passed over me took control like nothing before. It was as if someone had reached out and was slowly squeezing my throat. My oxygen disappeared, bit by bit. A random movie scene came to mind. The patient is immobilized on a ventilator when the villain enters and twists the oxygen tube, cutting off the oxygen supply. I tried to fight for my breath, but I was about to suffocate and die.

My hands trembled as I looked at my phone. I was supposed to call Shweta. I was supposed to reassure her that everything would be fine, but such assurances were no longer possible. I wanted to tell her that the raids were in an area of Taisoun where neither Nitu nor Mashi would ever go. She deserved that kind of comfort, but I could not give it to her. There was no way to sugarcoat the situation. Who would even believe me? I glanced at the mirrored art arrangement on the wall next to the dining table and recoiled at my reflection. My face was white as a sheet and my eyes were enlarged and sunken. I was going into shock as I struggled to take control. I might have lost the battle if you had not appeared next to me.

"Pishi, amar khide paache." *Auntie, I'm hungry.*

I managed to go into the kitchen and cut up an apple for you without slicing off a finger, but my hands shook again as soon as I put down the knife. After another attempt to reach both Mashi and Nitu, I returned Shweta's call.

"Naina, where have you been?"

I sighed. "I've been trying to reach them over the phone."

"Any luck?"

"No."

"What about where the raids happened? Could they really have been there?" I detected a trace of hope in her voice and grimaced as I squashed it.

"Shweta, I don't know. Mashi's house is in Om Tais where one of the attacks happened." My voice caught. "But it's a huge suburb. I didn't recognize any of the buildings on the news."

"I'm coming over there."

After the line went dead, I closed my eyes and a series of images flashed through my mind. The few memories I had of Nitu played like a high-speed slide show. I could hear his voice in the background. *Naina didi, I have to do this.* There was so much blame to go around. *Why did he have to go to East Africa during this turmoil? Why did Mashi let it happen?* She could have met us in Calcutta. *Why didn't Faisal refuse my request? Why did I facilitate Nitu's visa? Why didn't I refuse to do it?*

My eyes drifted to the couch where you sat with your computer. I glanced again at the mirror now behind you and I shuddered. My reflection still startled me.

I don't know how long I gaped blankly at the mirror, but I stopped when I felt something on my leg. I looked down to see that you'd come over to me and wrapped your arms around it. You could tell that I was upset—of course, you didn't know why—and you found a simple way to comfort me. My heart melted. I picked you up and held you close. You leaned into my chest, and within a few moments, you were fast asleep. I don't know how you knew that gesture would help me, but you did. Empathy was natural for you, even then.

****

By the time Shweta arrived, you'd comforted me through the initial shock. She made us tea while I put you back to bed. I settled on the couch with my phone and the cup of tea she had made for me.

"Nikhil's asleep?" she asked.

"Yeah," I confirmed.

"What should we do?"

"I don't know. I'm just going to keep trying them on the phone."

I retried all of the East African numbers I had, including Faisal's. Every ten minutes, I would redial one of the numbers. Shweta reached for the remote, turned on the news, and moved over to sit next to me. She grabbed one of my hands while we watched the updates unfold. My mind blocked out most of it, but I can remember bits and pieces.

"…death toll is rising…"

"Reports from two hospitals in Om Tais…emergency rooms operating well beyond capacity…"

"Clashes continue in northern Taisoun as recovery efforts in Om Tais are underway…"

The news reports were mixed intermittently with other sounds that reverberated through my mind. Blood pounding in my ears. Nitu's voice reading you a story. An M16 being fired—the spree of successive cracks that surpasses everything else in the surrounding ambiance. I'd heard that sound once at a gun range that Dev took me to before I went to Kabul. He wanted me to have a basic understanding of how to fire a gun if I ever needed to do so. We spent the day there, but I could never get used to the sound. In my imagination, that was the sound echoing between the buildings in Om Tais.

We tried to reach them a few more times on the phone, and at some point, my body granted me mercy. I slept until Shweta shook me awake two hours later.

"Naina, your phone is ringing," she hissed at me.

I fumbled to grab it. "Hello?"

"Naina, it's Mashi."

"Oh, thank God." My body shot up like a rod, all of my grogginess suddenly gone. "Mashi! Thank God. We've been trying to reach you all day. Are you okay? What happened?"

"I'm at the hospital."

Since Mashi was a doctor, her being at the hospital was generally not an indication of alarm, but something about her tone made my throat tighten. "What happened?"

"Tareq and Nitu were out for an early morning walk when I heard shots being fired."

By that point, I could hear her tone more clearly. She was crying. I tried to slow my breathing as I waited for her to finish.

"Tareq is okay—just a broken collarbone from the dive to the ground."

"And Nitu?" My throat threatened to constrict further.

"He's in the ICU. They are trying to relieve the pressure on his spinal cord."

"No," I gasped. A shiver passed through my body, and Shweta gripped my hand tightly.

"Naina, he spoke to Tareq before his surgery. I think he wants to see you."

He wants to see me. My body was rigid in shock. "He wants to see me?" I managed to whisper. My mind was running at a hundred miles an hour now. *What should I do?* I knew enough about biology to know that Nitu might not have much time left. The surgery could go well and he might be fine, but the risks were incredibly high. I still had a valid visa for East Africa, and no one else would be able to go. By the time a new visa could be processed, the airports would be closed, or worse, Nitu could be dead.

"Yes, he does. Naina, I'm sorry to make this so quick, but I have to go. I have to check on Tareq, but my phone should be working now. Let me know what you decide to do. I'll call you with any updates on Nitu." She sniffled loudly.

"Love you, Mashi." The words came pouring out of me before I could stop to think about them. I had never said that to her before.

At first, I wasn't sure if she'd noticed, but her response came back quickly. "Love you too, betu."

I just sat there, stunned and immobile, with the phone at my ear for several moments. Shweta was staring at me, but I could not speak. The words would simply not form—in my head or on my tongue. She put her arm around my shoulder and waited patiently. I don't think I could have been so patient had the roles been reversed.

I must have opened my mouth and closed it a couple of times before she squeezed my wrist and whispered. "What happened?"

I swallowed loudly. "Nitu's in the hospital. He had some kind of spinal cord injury. He's in surgery now."

"What else did she say?"

I leaned back into the couch with my eyes closed. When my eyes shot open a moment later, I had my answer. "I have to go see him."

Shweta gawked at me as she gestured toward the television. "What are you talking about? Didn't you just see how dangerous it is?"

I stood up, went into my room, and began throwing things into a small duffle bag. "I know it's crazy. I know it's going to be dangerous. But I have to go. I can't not go. He asked for me. Somebody needs to be there, and I'm the only one who can make the trip."

I ignored her expression and grabbed my phone to call Faisal. Since Mashi's phone was working now, I hoped his would be too. He picked up after one ring.

"Naina, I don't have much time."

"Are you okay? Arya?"

"Thankfully we're both fine. I can't believe she and her parents decided to come back from Ethiopia this week. I'm trying to get them out of the country right now. Have you spoken to your aunt and cousin? I tried them this morning, but didn't get through."

"Yeah."

He could probably hear the break in my voice. "What happened?"

"Nitu's in the hospital. He's having spinal cord decompression surgery."

"Holy sh—"

"F-Faisal, I'm leaving for Taisoun. Today. As soon as possible."

I could almost hear the thud of his jaw drop on the other side of the line. "What the h—? Are you, er, are you sure?" *Are you insane?* He didn't have to say it—I knew that he was thinking it.

"I have to. I know it's crazy, but I have to do this. Someone needs to be there, and I'm the only one with a valid East African visa."

"But his mother is with him. And isn't she a doctor? She can care for him better than anyone can. Stay in Calcutta."

"I can't do that."

"Damn it, Naina," Faisal replied tersely and sighed. "Damn your hard head and that valid visa."

"So you'll be there tomorrow?"

"If you're really doing this, of course I'll be there. Text me your flight info. I'll pick you up with a UN detail."

I exhaled loudly. "Thank you. Thank you so much, Faisal."

Two hours later, I boarded a flight to Doha that connected me to Taisoun. I arrived there just in time. Within forty-eight hours, the East African government closed the airports.

****

June, 2017 – My arrival in Taisoun

A slow-moving, exhausted Faisal awaited me at the airport when I arrived in Taisoun at four in the morning the following day. I remember the initial shock when I walked up to the customs booths. Instead of the usual crowd pushing through the lines, the airport was desolate. Three customs agents sat at their booths, but there were only two other visitors besides myself. There was an unnerving calm hovering over the scene—the eye of the storm. I tried not to dwell on that and passed through security without any issues.

Faisal simply patted me on the shoulder instead of the usual hug. We exchanged glances, and I realized what he was trying to say. We'd be saving any personal greetings for when we were in private. Instead of the car that he had driven last time, we boarded the back of a black panel van. He slid the door shut and let out a sigh of relief as the driver steered the van toward the exit.

"Thanks for picking me up," I said with a hug. "How are you doing?"

"I don't know." Faisal shook his head. "Things are so tense. I don't know what to do. I finally got Arya and her parents onto a flight last night. They flew out to visit family in Dubai."

"I'm glad you managed to get them out."

"You and me both. Arya's dad is the most stubborn person on the planet. Anyway, he decided he didn't want to leave again, blah blah. When they went to Ethiopia before, it was just supposed to be a vacation, so he accepted that trip. But he didn't want to flee his own country. God, he drives me crazy. I can see where she gets her obstinate streak from."

"I'm glad he agreed," I said with a smile. "When are you getting married?"

"I don't know. We're officially engaged now. That's as far as I need to be involved. They can do the planning and tell me where and when to show up." He looked away, embarrassed, but I could see that his face was beaming.

My eyes lit up. "Don't you dare try to hide that smile. I'm so excited for you both. Congratulations."

"Thanks. Maybe by the time we get married, this firestorm will have cleared." Faisal gestured toward the side of the van, obviously to the turmoil outside, but there was no window. "Have you heard anything about Nitu's surgery?"

"Not yet. When I boarded my flight in Calcutta, he was just going into the second surgery. The first one went okay. I'm not sure what else needs to happen. I guess Mashi will explain it."

"Was their home hit in the raid?" Faisal asked. "I thought they lived in a different part of Om Tais."

"They do," I sighed. "Nitu and Mashi's husband, Tareq, chose yesterday of all days to go for an early morning walk."

"Bloody hell." Faisal's eyes widened. "I'm so sorry." He reached out and put his arm around my shoulder. "It's going to be okay."

My torso shook as I stared straight ahead. Tears were a luxury that I could not afford, not while I could still control them. At some point, I knew they would overwhelm my defenses, but not yet. "I hope so."

I glanced around the blank walls of the van, seeking any form of distraction. "Are you still driving your car?" I asked him.

"No. Two weeks ago, the UN issued an advisory, so we aren't llowed to drive our cars anymore. We've all had to switch to only ısing the UN's armored vehicles with trained defensive drivers. For rips like this one, preferably vans without windows."

"I thought the UN traveled in white vans with 'United Nations' vritten on the side?"

Faisal nodded. "We used to, but they got rid of those in the past ouple of years. It was too risky—basically a huge sign that said 'we ıave expats on board,' rather than 'we are an impartial party,' which s what they were going for."

"I see."

"Yeah, you know, since the UN is so well regarded verywhere."

That brought a short-lived smile onto my face. "Indeed."

"So we have another half hour before we get to the hospital. It's on the far side of Om Tais. Do you want to take a rest?"

"That's probably a good idea." I closed my eyes for a second and then forced them open. "Faisal, I'm not sure if I said it enough lready, but thank you. You've been an amazing help. I don't know vhat I would've done without you."

"What are friends for?" he responded. "Try to get some rest."

****

Faisal woke me up when we were pulling into the hospital parking ot. "Naina, we're here," he said as he shook my shoulder.

My eyes fluttered open. We got out of the van and walked straight to the waiting room. Mashi sat in the back corner. She'd buried her face in her hands and her curly hair had gone radial, as if she'd just been through one of those static electricity science fair experiments that I took you to see as a child. As an engineer, I'm sure you know how that works better than I do.

I walked up to her unsteadily and touched her shoulder. "Hi Mashi," I whispered.

She looked up and an expression of gratitude spread across her face as I sat down next to her and she put her arms around me.

A moment later, I gestured toward Faisal and reintroduced them. "This is my friend Faisal who works with the UN here. He arranged for Nitu's visa."

She gave him a watery smile and shook his hand, after which Faisal gave us a quick nod and excused himself. "Please let me know if there's any help that you need. My best wishes go with both of you. Naina, give me a call later, okay?"

"I will. Thank you."

After he left, I took a seat next to Mashi. "How are you? Tell me about what's going on."

She scrutinized the wall behind me as she answered. "Tareq is fine. Our driver took him home to take a shower and change. He has a small, aligned fracture of the collarbone, so it should heal on its own. His arm is in a sling, and he'll need to ice his collarbone regularly. They gave him a prescription for some pain meds in case he needs it, but he'll probably only want to take ibuprofen or acetaminophen. He should be back in the next half hour or so." She wrung her hands together. "Nitu made it through the night, but they took him back into surgery this morning."

"What happened to them in the raid?"

She shook her head. "I don't know. He and Tareq were out walking. Tareq said there was a large blast that knocked them both out. When he came to a few moments later, he found Nitu unconscious under a pile of rubble."

"The blast blew them apart?"

"Yes." Mashi's shoulders shook, and I put my arm over them. "We were able to talk to him again last night. He was happy when I told him you were coming here."

I forced the corners of my mouth upward a bit. It felt as if there were a haze over everything in the waiting room while we waited for an update. The hospital looked remarkably well run compared to what was reported on the news. There were people everywhere, though, and the atmosphere was heavy, morose, and tearful.

I remember trying to read a book. I turned the pages of chapter after chapter, but when I picked the book up again later in the week, my memory of it was blank. I ended up rereading everything that I supposedly read that day in the waiting room.

Tareq arrived sometime later. I spoke to him briefly when he joined us in the waiting room. We sat there in a row, gawping without noticing a single thing. I tried to exchange some pleasantries with him, but whatever he said in return went in one ear and out the other. I did, however, notice his condition. He held his right arm close to his torso because of the sling and his face had some minor cuts and bruises. He moved slowly and was clearly in a lot of pain, but his injuries were minor, as Mashi had said.

I was grateful that he had pulled Nitu out of the rubble, but at the same time, I was resentful. His foolishness is what had kept Mashi in East Africa during such turmoil. Had they not been so stubborn about leaving during the turmoil, Nitu would never have gone to East Africa. I knew Tareq's presence was comforting to Mashi, but I wanted him to leave. I barely knew how to interact with her, and his appearance only complicated things further. *Was I being selfish?* She did have the right to move on, to build a new life. She had the right to be happy, but why did she have to forget about her other family in the process? Why did she drive her son to take such a huge risk? How could she allow him to even think about risking so much after everything she'd already put him through, much less act on the impulse?

Nitu was in surgery, and I'd come to be there for him, in a country about to implode. Would it be the last time I saw Nitu alive? And if he died, what would happen to you?

The thought of you brought me a moment of happiness. I pictured myself setting you up at your computer. I could feel you hugging my leg when you noticed I was upset. Bouncing you on my lap. Those images brought me some momentary respite until the doctor approached to speak to us.

He spoke in Arabic, and my rudimentary knowledge was just enough to pick up a few critical phrases. "Not out of danger yet…some bad injuries…next day…"

Mashi thanked him and they walked away together. They must have been discussing all of the gory medical details. I watched them from my seat and relief overcame me as I noticed a glimpse of the same sentiment on her face.

"We can go see him in about an hour. He should be awake by then," Mashi said when she returned.

"What did he say? I only picked up some bits and pieces."

"The surgery went all right. He still has a number of abrasions, and they hope the stitches will hold. The next day will be critical."

"Mashi, can you explain what happened to him? Medically, I mean."

When she didn't respond, Tareq nudged her and she looked up. "I'm sorry, Naina. What did you say?"

"Could you explain what the operations are for? What happened to him—medically, that is?"

"The rubble he landed under caused some internal bleeding and injuries to his spinal cord. They've been trying to decompress and stabilize the spinal cord, and then address the bleeding."

I nodded and leaned back against the wall behind my chair. I don't think I moved for at least an hour. That's when a nurse came by to tell us that Nitu was awake. She took us in one visitor at a time.

****

Since I hadn't seen Nitu after my arrival in East Africa, Mashi let me go in to see him first. I don't know what I expected. I hadn't, and thankfully still haven't, spent a large amount of time in hospitals. Until that moment, I'd never had to visit someone after an almost fatal accident; I had visited friends and family after scheduled operations or giving birth, but nothing close to what Nitu went through. The only experience that I had to go on was what I'd seen on television, which was nothing like reality.

As the nurse led me to the room, she warned me against having an outward reaction to his appearance. "It will only make him feel worse," she stressed.

I nodded and mentally repeated that to prep myself. When we reached the doorway, I stopped and took a deep breath. I could already smell the deep-seated scent of antiseptic, and my apprehension grew by the second.

My first thought after getting a glimpse of him was, *That's not so bad.* A nurse was resting an ice pack on his heavily bandaged right leg, covered in bruising and abrasions. A sheet covered the rest of his body with his face peeking out. It was battered and discolored, but I could still see his eyes.

As I took in the scene, it required all of my willpower to stop the tears from flowing. I had seen worse medical scenes on TV, but those didn't involve Nitu. Those fictional patients weren't my flesh and blood. His face stood out in such contrast to the white pillow beneath him that I shuddered. The bruising had left his face in three shades of dark red.

I focused on his eyes as I approached. "Hey, buddy." I reached out and gave his hand a gentle squeeze.

He wore a neck brace, so he couldn't turn his head, but his eyes flitted toward me. "Th-th-thank you f-for coming here," he said in a raspy voice.

"Where else would I be?" My tone was unsteady, but I managed to get the words out.

"It, it's dangerous…to be here." He took a deep breath and his voice started to even out. "But I wanted you to come. Sorry I didn't listen, Naina didi."

I leaned over so that he could see me more easily. "No apologies. I'm glad that I'm here, okay?"

"O-okay."

There was a chair by the window, so I pulled it close to the bed. "How are you feeling? You look like a champ."

"Ah, it hurts too much to laugh," he croaked.

"All right. Then tell me how you're feeling. For real."

"I'm fine." His eyes glazed over. "You're crazy. I'm f-fine." Nitu pressed the button to administer a dose of morphine to his IV drip and squinted. "The TV. It has pretty colors…"

Got to love morphine.

His voice continued to drone on. "Do you think, do you think I'm a good f-father?" he continued. "I'm such a bad son." He looked away, "I don't know how to talk to my own mother…"

"Nikhil's doing fine. Don't worry about him. Shweta's taking good care of him."

"I should have gotten to know you better. Naina didi, will you get to know me?"

"I will, don't worry."

"I'm sorry that we won't get the chance. You might have to take care of Nikhil for a long time."

I pulled the sides of my black cardigan closer together and crossed my arms as I leaned forward. "Nitu, what are you talking about? The doctor said that you're doing fine."

"Didn't want to tell you…didn't know, wasn't sure…I'm sick…"

"What? Nitu?"

I sighed as I realized that he'd passed out. On my way back to the waiting room, I frowned as I considered what he had said. What did he mean about being sick? *Must have been the drugs talking.* I decided not to mention it to Mashi because it would only make her worry more.

****

Mashi sat with Nitu for a while, but he didn't stir again that day. I was in the waiting room when Faisal came by to offer me a ride home. "You can drop off your stuff and get cleaned up."

I made sure that the disposable phone I'd purchased on my previous trip to East Africa was working, and we set off to Mashi's house. "Thanks again, Faisal. You've been a godsend," I said as I climbed into a black SUV with dark tinted windows instead of the van we had taken from the airport.

"All in a day's work. How's he doing? Did he get out of surgery okay?"

"So far so good." I shut my eyes for a moment. "He looks terrible, but I guess it'll heal." A surge of relief passed over me as I felt the brave face I'd been putting on fall away. "I'm sorry, it's not as if you don't have enough to deal with already." I wiped the tears off my cheeks with my palms, begging them to stop as they came down with relentless fury.

Faisal handed me a tissue box. We sat in silence for the first ten minutes of the ride as I fought to reclaim control over my emotions.

"Thank you," I said as I blew my nose.

"It's okay, Naina. Better to let yourself feel it than to bottle it all up."

"Maybe." I took a few sips from the bottle of water I had procured while at the hospital. "Let's talk about something else. How are Arya and her family doing?"

Faisal's expression brightened. "Arya loves Dubai as much as any shopaholic. I'm happy to let her get that trip out of her system while she's still on her father's credit card." He shrugged. "They're fine, but they're worried about things here."

"And I'll bet she's worried about you."

"You're right, she is. I'll be okay, though. Most of the staff is already gone, but I volunteered to be in the small contingent that stayed."

I bit down on my lip. "I didn't realize they were evacuating you."

"All nonessential staff members were moved out weeks ago, but yeah, they did ask me to leave. Yesterday." He glanced out the window. "I volunteered to stay."

"Oh." I felt the guilt weigh heavily on my shoulders once again. I knew that part of the reason he was staying was because of me. I was tempted to say something, to tell him that he shouldn't put himself at risk, but the words would not come. We both knew that my family needed him, and he was too good of a friend, of a person, to leave us in the lurch. "What do you think is going to happen here?"

Faisal shook his head. "I have no idea. I think Bahtez will have to resign, but what happens after is anyone's guess. Things could get pretty chaotic, if my country is any example."

I sighed. "Let's hope things calm down faster here than they did in Egypt."

We arrived at Mashi's house five minutes later. The driver parked in the gated garage, and I was about to open the door when Faisal caught my hand. "Naina, I want you to move out of the car and into the house as quickly as possible. We shouldn't be outside." He reached over the seat and grabbed my suitcase as I pulled the keys out of my pocket.

As soon as the car door opened, I darted straight to the front door and began to unlock it. Faisal was a couple of steps behind me when we felt it.

I heard a thud in the distance and noticed a cloud of dust escaping into the sky in my peripheral vision. "What was tha—?"

I started to turn around to see what it was, but Faisal pushed me into the house and slammed the door behind us.

I fell forward and landed on my hands and knees. "What was that?"

His face looked grim. "Another bomb." He drew the shutters across the glass door and started to draw the shades and drapes for the windows downstairs. "I didn't think there were going to be any more raids today."

"What should we do?"

Once he'd secured all of the windows in our immediate vicinity, he answered, "We should stay inside for a while."

"But I need to get back to the hospital. Nitu needs me."

"You won't do him any good if you're dead or injured. That bomb wasn't far from here. We can't leave right now."

A shiver passed through me. *Maybe I should have listened to Dev.* I gritted my teeth. "Okay. I'm going to go take a shower then."

"Go for it. Naina, is it okay for Jamal to come inside too? I don't want him waiting out in the car."

"I'm so sorry. I should've said so. Of course he can come inside."

"It's okay. Go take a shower, maybe take a nap, and then we can head back to the hospital if it seems clear."

Before I grabbed my suitcase, I ran to Faisal and hugged him. "Thank you."

After my shower, I lay down in one of the guest rooms upstairs and, as soon as my head touched the pillow, I fell asleep. Faisal had said that he would wake me when the situation was calmer. I had hoped that would mean we'd be there only a few hours, but it turned out that we couldn't return to the hospital until the next day.

****

June, 2017 – The hospital bed

"Naina, wake up. We can go back to the hospital now," someone hissed at me. I heard the whisper in my dream.

"Wha-what's going on?" I mumbled. My eyes fluttered open. The room was dark with the shades drawn, so it was easy to close them again. "I'm so tired," I said as I rolled over.

"Come on. We should get back now," I heard again.

The hospital. The words started to compute in my mind. *The hospital. Nitu. We have to get back to the hospital.* My eyes snapped open. "Shit, yes. Let's go."

I crawled out of bed and fumbled through getting dressed and brushing my teeth. When I walked into the kitchen ten minutes later, Faisal handed me a thermos full of tea. After the first three sips, I felt as if I'd returned to Earth.

"You changed clothes?" I noticed.

The left side of his face crinkled, showing off a prominent dimple. "You were sleeping for a while. I had some clothes in the car. I don't go anywhere without a bag of essentials these days."

"Have you heard anything from Mashi?"

"I called to tell her what happened yesterday and to make sure she had my phone number. She spent the night at the hospital to keep an eye on Nitu. She wanted you to stay here and get some rest, and I wanted to wait until things stabilized."

I was about to protest when I remembered. *Right. The bomb blast. Somewhere nearby.* "So you stayed here last night?"

"Yeah. She said it was okay, so I went ahead and made myself at home. Jamal went home to his family. He'll be here with the car in the next ten minutes or so."

"Did she say anything about Nitu's condition?"

Faisal shook his head. "No, but she did say that her husband would come back here at some point." He shrugged his shoulders. "I never heard him come in last night, so I texted her to ask if he was still with her. She said that he decided to spend the night at the hospital too."

My eyes noticed that the couch had been moved so that Faisal could sleep on it while keeping his eyes on the door. *Wow.* My jaw clenched when I thought of Tareq. *Damned husband. All of this because of that stupid early morning walk.* With a deep breath, I tried to remind myself that the accident was no one's fault.

I knew that rationally. No one could have predicted what would have happened that morning, especially in the suburban neighborhood Mashi and Tareq called home. I just wanted someone to blame, and Tareq was the easiest target. I hadn't bonded with him, so I didn't feel guilty about sending the blame his way. That's what Nitu must have been trying to do by going out on the walk—bond with Tareq. I was sure of it. He'd never shown any inclination for early morning walks in Calcutta. I sighed. *If only they hadn't gone out that day.*

"You okay?" Faisal asked. "You don't look so good."

I shook off my thoughts and took a seat at the table in the kitchen. "I never drink coffee, but I swear, today I need it."

"Okay." He dumped the tea out of the thermos and handed me a fresh cup.

About five minutes later, we heard the car outside and rushed off to the hospital.

****

When we walked into the waiting room, there was no sign of Mashi or Tareq. "They must be in his room," I said.

"Go ahead. I'm going to head to the office. I'll give you a call later, okay?"

"Thank you. Be safe." As soon as he was gone, I went to Nitu's room.

The first thing I noticed was that his face didn't look quite as gruesome as the previous day. Some color that wasn't a byproduct of the bruises and lacerations had appeared on his cheeks. The scene remained ugly and fearsome, but the improvement was still noticeable. I walked to the bed and gave him the best sort of hug that I could with the position he was in.

"You look pretty handsome this morning," I said with a smile.

"Bet the girls would be swooning." His voice sounded more relaxed and less raspy than the day before.

My eyes brightened when I glanced at Mashi and Tareq as they sat in hard plastic chairs placed on the other side of Nitu's bed. "Good morning. How are you both?" I focused my gaze on Tareq. "Faisal said that you were supposed to come home last night but you decided to stay. Is everything all right? Are you okay?"

Tareq nodded. "I'm fine. My collarbone is the same, not much better but not any worse. They offered us cots last night, so I decided to stay here with Trina."

"Oh, I see." I nodded and watched as he put his uninjured left arm around Mashi's shoulders. Mashi smiled at him and patted his leg, but she had turned back toward Nitu when I noticed Tareq wince and then gingerly remove his arm from around her shoulders.

Sleeping on a cot had to be miserable with his injury, and now he's sitting in the world's most uncomfortable chair. But he did it for Mashi. That was probably the moment when my opinion of Tareq began to change.

"How are things back at the house? Your friend said there was an explosion nearby?" Mashi asked.

I pursed my lips. "I don't really know what happened, but everything seems fine now. No disturbances during the night either."

The worry on her face abated slightly. "I'm so glad. Tell Faisal thank you for me. It was really nice of him to stay with you yesterday."

"He's definitely a sweetheart," I agreed.

"He's done so much for you. And for all of us. Such a wonderful man." I could tell what she was hinting at, but I refused to acknowledge it.

"He's been a great friend, and we go back a long way. He'd walk through fire for any of his friends or family. You should hear about everything he's gone through to keep his fiancée and her family safe." I turned toward Nitu and squeezed his hand. "I'm going to go call Dev and also check on stuff in Calcutta. I'll be back in right after that, okay?"

"Of course," he nodded.

On the way out of the room, I dialed Shweta's number so that I could talk to you. I considered asking Nitu if he wanted to speak to you directly, but I wasn't sure about what to do in front of Mashi. As far as I could tell, he still hadn't told her about you yet, so I kept my mouth shut.

I spoke to you for about five minutes. The first time that we tried using video chat when I was back in Paris, you tapped the screen as if you could reach through it and touch my face. Once I came back to Calcutta, I started reading you the first *Harry Potter* books aloud in the evenings. I wanted to tell you stories that you hadn't heard before, and I didn't know what Nitu had already read to you. You were so engrossed and excited. I'm not sure how much you really understood, but given how much you still love those books, I think you understood more than we thought at the time. We explained that the magical iPad that I had given to Shweta was like one of those special pictures from the books. It was a way for me to always be with you.

On the video chat, you showed me a new Lego building that you had constructed, mumbling around, and then I watched you break the top half to rebuild it. You were already an engineer, even as a child.

Shweta and I also spoke for a couple of minutes. We discussed having you speak to Nitu via video chat, but decided the trauma might be too great. Would you recognize him in his current state? Would you understand that he was badly hurt? Since I couldn't discuss it with Nitu alone, I felt a bit lost. I remember wondering if that was what it felt like to be a parent. That lost feeling returned to me often while you and your sister were growing up. The "right" path often eludes us. I'm sure you'll understand when your own time comes. I can hardly believe that it will be so soon.

So Shweta and I decided to wait to put you on video chat until the bruises on Nitu's face subsided. My biggest fear was that you wouldn't recognize him. I could not even imagine how much that would have hurt him. Thankfully, I never had to find out.

****

Later that day, I managed to get some time alone with Nitu. I was grateful that he'd remained lucid, and I wanted to take advantage of it.

We didn't talk much about what he'd said the day before.

"How was it? Taking care of Nikhil?" he asked.

I beamed when I thought of you. You were the only high point in my day. "He's wonderful. Everyone loves him. He's getting bigger you know. I know he can't wait to see his dad again."

"Sure."

Nitu's face looked crestfallen, so I showed him some pictures on my phone. There was one of the two of us together that Shweta had taken, and another of you at your learning computer. We took a family shot with you and Shweta's parents, and one with you and Sameer Mama fast asleep on the couch with your mouths open. The pictures made him miss you more, but still lightened both of our moods.

"Is he still doing the finger painting?" Nitu inquired.

"Yeah, but he's also into drawing these days. He has a good eye." As the daughter of architects, I immediately noticed that about your drawings. Your perspective has served you well as an engineer.

"Maybe he gets that from you, from your side of our family," he said.

I chuckled at the thought. "Tell me about things with you and Mashi. How was it going? You know, before all of this?" I gestured around the hospital room.

"It's okay. She still feels far away." His face darkened. "And I'm angry at her. I feel as if she should apologize for how much she screwed up my life, but she hasn't said anything. If she's not going to explain why she left, then she at least owes me an apology. I don't know how to get past that."

"What did she say?"

"Same stuff as before," he answered. "Like in the letter. She wants to get to know me, to be a part of my life now. But I don't know if I can let her."

I tilted my head to the side. "But you came all this way? I didn't realize you felt that way."

"I wanted to try."

"I think it takes time," I countered. "There's no magic cure. And I think it's just hard for her. To say that she's sorry means she has to relive all of the reasons why she needs to apologize. I guess she wants to start over with a blank slate, but it's not that easy for any of us, especially you. We want an explanation about the past, and she just wants to move forward."

"You forgave her, didn't you?"

I let out a long exhale and leaned away from him. "I don't know. I guess so. Mostly. But she isn't my mother."

"So?"

"Everything between us is different." I shrugged. "I didn't have to forgive her for as much as you will. She was never supposed to be there for me every day, but she was supposed to be there for you. She was supposed to put you first, even above herself and everything else. She didn't leave me the same way she abandoned you. I'm not angry with her, but I understand why you would be, why you are."

"Thanks, Naina didi. I've been trying, but I'm struggling with it and I don't know where it's going. I still haven't even told her about Nikhil. I was tempted to show her pictures, but I couldn't bring it up."

"Do you want me to tell her about him?

Nitu hesitated. "No. She should hear it from me. I just have to figure out how she fits into my life and if I can trust her before I can trust her with Nikhil. I won't let her break his heart. He's the most important thing in the world to me."

I agreed with him, but I knew that he had no real plan to tell her anything at that point. Mashi still hadn't earned Nitu's trust, and it would take time to do that.

****

During the following week, we developed something of a routine. Mashi's neighborhood in Om Tais was calmer, so we were able to go home in shifts using Tareq's car. Faisal would come by to check on me occasionally, and we even made plans for dinner a couple of times. Mashi promised to have him over as soon as we took Nitu home from the hospital. She wanted to thank him for everything he'd done for all of us.

The moments that I spent with your Uncle Faisal were a godsend. We'd known each other for so long that I didn't feel pressured to carry a conversation and the contrast was clear. I still had so much trouble being alone with Tareq during our short drives home from the hospital. My mind would freeze up or my throat would turn dry. Small talk was simply impossible for me. I could never bring myself to focus on getting to know him; in my head, I was still at the hospital, at home in Paris with Dev, or in Calcutta with you sitting on my lap. He was nice enough, and I could see that he treated Mashi well. She lit up in his presence with a radiance that I'd never seen when I spent time with her alone. Despite that, I regressed into a sullen teenager stuck in lunch detention whenever it was just the two of us.

My interactions with Mashi had improved dramatically, at least when we were alone, or just with Nitu. We found ourselves in real conversations about family, and about movies and East Africa, topics important and unimportant. At some point, our smiles stopped being forced and we were able to joke and laugh together. There were occasional reminders that we barely knew each other, but they were few and far between as we became more familiar with each other. At times like that, there might be an awkward silence until someone broke the tension in time for the ambiance to return to normal—our version of normal. The relationship was a work in progress, but the pain associated with it had begun to subside.

****

After weeks of putting it off, I finally told my mom what I was doing in East Africa. The shock in her voice was palpable, even over the shaky Skype connection. I could see the emotions on her face developing slowly as my words sank in. In spite of that, she mentioned none of her pain, hurt, or anger.

"That's amazing—that you found her. Is Nitu okay?" She said it twice. "I wish you'd told me before, that you hadn't felt the need to keep it from me." I could tell how hurt she was by what I did. More than anything, I'd brought old emotions to the surface that she'd long ago bottled up—anger, pain, and fear. Why had Mashi seemingly forgotten all of us? What had happened to her? How could she abandon her own son?

The next day, Mom called me. Our conversation was stilted until she asked to speak to Mashi. I was relieved that she asked, so I set them up on video chat. To give them some privacy, I retreated to take a shower. I wanted to keep my distance from what I expected would be a tense conversation.

At least I pretended to do that. In reality, I took a seat in the next room to eavesdrop on the conversation.

"Hi, Bia didi," Mashi said to my mom, using her daak nam.

"Hi, Trina."

"It's been so long," Mashi said in Bengali.

Mom ignored the sentiment and changed the subject. "How is Nitu? Naina said that he's in the hospital?"

"He's doing okay. Much better. It was touch and go for a while, but he's doing much better."

"Good."

"How is Diptu?" Mashi asked about my dad, using the nickname that he'd had back in college.

"He's fine. We're both in New York, helping out with wedding planning for Naina. I came over here a while ago, but he joined me this month after his project in London ended." Mom's voice was short and rigid, obviously trying to hide all of the emotion brewing underneath the surface.

"That's good. Maybe you both could come visit me here sometime."

"Let's see how the situation develops."

"Yes."

"Anyway, Trina, I have to go. Naina asked me to run some errands for the wedding. I have to get to the shop before it closes."

"Oh, of course." I could hear the disappointment in Mashi's voice through the door.

"Bye."

My mom hung up, and that was it. No fireworks. No yelling. No tears. Just tension and silence. I had thought things were awkward between Tareq and me, but they definitely had us beat. Over the years since then, they've started to chip away at it, but they're still not through all of the baggage from that time.

****

I'm behind now with writing all of this out for you. I had planned to have already given you this account by now. Since you came over last month and told us that our grandchild is a girl, I've been unable to focus on writing. Time has disappeared as I've shopped online for baby clothes and rattles, cribs and décor for the nursery. Today I spent three hours on the Babies "R" Us website browsing their inventory of toys and clothing.

I promised myself that I would give this to you before the baby is born. I want my conscience to be clear the first time I hold my beautiful little granddaughter. So here I go, with the sprint to the finish. This is the hardest part. Every word seems daunting, but no amount of procrastination will make this any easier to write, so I must trudge on.

****

A few days after that first awkward conversation between Mashi and Mom, things seemed to take a turn for the better. Nitu's condition had improved considerably. He still couldn't be released from the hospital, but he was able to move around. He sat in a wheelchair that I pushed to the vending machine down the hall from his room—a welcome sight after so many days cooped up in bed. Nitu resented the chair, but he was trying to make the best of it.

Some days were better than others. I could tell that he yearned to be outside. If the situation in Taisoun had been less risky, I would have taken him for a stroll around the hospital grounds. The first day I wheeled him around inside, he was excited, but on the second day, he was crabby and withdrawn. I couldn't blame him, of course, because anyone in his situation would have succumbed to cabin fever much earlier. By that time, he'd been living in the hospital for more than three weeks.

Since the initial round of surgeries, he had undergone several more minor procedures. I don't remember the details. I'm sure that Mashi explained them to me a number of times, but most of it never made it into my thick skull. That's the reason he couldn't leave the hospital. There was always another procedure or another issue—a never ending slew of treatments.

The truth is that the treatments weren't working. I'm not sure when I began to realize that. Nitu was recovering from many of his injuries, but he had yet to regain most of the sensation in his legs. The decompression procedure of his spinal cord had kept the nerves alive, but his recovery was slower than it should have been.

The doctors kept it from him—or so I thought—because he still had some sensation there. They were hoping to save him from being bound to the wheelchair for good. I don't know if Mashi knew or not. My guess is that they told her the situation, but that she blocked it out or was in denial. Whatever the reason, she refused to acknowledge it. Letting her analytical mind touch on those possibilities was too real. She didn't want to believe that her son might never walk again.

To be honest, I think that I knew too. It irked me that Nitu wasn't trying to stand up. Why wasn't he going in for physical therapy? Those questions appeared in the recesses of my mind, but I pushed them aside. Who was I to question the doctors? What did I know about recovery from surgery?

I sensed Nitu's growing frustration, but I didn't know how to help him get through it. I stood with him at the vending machine, and day after day, I asked him what kind of soda he wanted. We didn't talk about how he felt or what the doctors had said to him about his prognosis—just his soda preferences.

Until my East Africa trip, you were the bridge that kept us talking, but now I wasn't even sure how to talk to him about you. He asked about you all the time, but something was different. I didn't understand why he didn't want to speak to you directly or hear me recount your most recent escapades I'd heard about from Shweta. It didn't occur to me what was going on until much later.

****

June, 2017 – Home from the hospital

A week later, we took Nitu home from the hospital. Once we'd set him up in the other guest room, I started making preparations for us to leave together. He'd progressed enough with his recovery that he could stand for a moment or two, but walking remained beyond his abilities.

The situation in Taisoun had subsided. Protests were ongoing but had lost their momentum following the military raids. People were too scared to risk another attack on a residential community, so their numbers had declined. They'd also shifted focus. Instead of calling for the president's resignation, they now called for better economic policy.

In spite of the relative calm, the tension in the air was still present. The government had reopened Taisoun's airport, but the majority of international flights had yet to resume. The airport was operating well below capacity while bookings were through the roof. Most of the online systems had crashed, so Faisal drove me to the airport one afternoon to book our tickets. We used an armored car rather than the fully secured black panel van.

As we drove to the airport, we discussed the potential consequences of the protests and the attempted revolution. "What do you think is going to happen?" I had to ask him three times before I could elicit a response.

"Bahtez is apparently setting up a more participatory government." I could see the look of disdain on his face.

"Do you believe that?"

"Nope, but I'd be happy to be wrong." Faisal sighed. "Arya and her parents are talking about coming back."

"Isn't that a good thing?"

"I don't know. Maybe," he shrugged. "I'm worried. My gut tells me that it's not over yet. I just don't know when it will start again."

Some part of me knew he was right. I wanted to be optimistic. I wanted to believe that the worst was behind us, but I also knew that human energy could only be suppressed for so long. The current calm could only be sustained until the energy of the revolution overflowed once again.

As you already know, it did.

****

When we reached the airport, I booked two tickets to Calcutta, with a connection through Doha. Every flight was overbooked, so the first booking that I could confirm was eight days away.

"I guess it's better than nothing," I grumbled as Faisal and I walked out of the airport.

"I'm going to make sure you get on that flight."

Something about the way he said it made me look at him in concern. I stepped up into the car and waited for him to join me. When the door was safely shut, I confronted him. "What did you mean just now? Is something going on?"

He kept his eyes on the window and frowned. Clearly, he didn't want to tell me whatever it was.

"Faisal, what is it?"

He hesitated. "I received a directive for orderly evacuation. They're pulling us all out at the end of next week. We have ten days to evacuate, but I hope to make it sooner. Since I volunteered to stay, I'll manage local staff evacuations, but I have to report to the office in Geneva right after that's completed."

The magnitude of what he was saying struck me slowly. "But I thought…I thought it was calmer now? I know we both think that things are going to get worse, but why would the UN evacuate its last staff after the tension has subsided?"

"I don't know," Faisal shook his head. "The higher-ups might know something that we don't. That's why I all but yelled at Arya to stay put in Dubai. And that's why I need to make sure that you get out before I have to leave. No more delays, okay?"

A shiver went up my spine. We were lucky that the airport had reopened. We couldn't miss this chance. "Yeah. Let's make sure of it."

I don't think we talked much for the rest of the drive. We were both too preoccupied. What was the UN expecting to happen? What did they know that we didn't? And what should I tell Mashi and Nitu? There had to be some way that I could convince Mashi and her husband to leave. *Would they consider leaving with us now?* I wondered. I had new information now. I had to convince them. They'd refused me staunchly so many times, but that was before all of this. Before the military raided Om Tais. Before the bomb blast that injured Nitu.

****

Later that night, Mashi and I were sitting by Nitu's bed. Tareq had already gone to bed, but the three of us were knee-deep in our own respective guilty pleasures. I was rereading a Frederick Forsyth novel on my iPad; Mashi was engrossed in some kind of romance story; and Nitu was pouring over an anthology of science fiction stories that I'd purchased for him at the Calcutta airport.

I looked up from my book and debated disturbing the momentary peace. *Should I bring it up? Is this a good time?* The debate in my mind raged as I tried to put off an uncomfortable conversation. The reality was that we were leaving in a week, and there would be no good time to explain that. So I plunged ahead.

"I bought tickets today." I hadn't told Mashi that Faisal was taking me to the airport.

"Tickets?" She looked up with raised eyebrows.

"Yes. Plane tickets. Nitu and I will be leaving at the end of next week." I shifted in my seat as I waited for her reaction.

"I see." Mashi took a deep breath and returned to her book.

Nitu and I exchanged a glance, so I decided to try again. "Mashi, we were wondering if you and Tareq would come with us."

She looked up at me again and blinked rapidly. I watched her closely, hoping to see some sign that she was considering the idea. A moment later, she crushed those hopes by shaking her head decisively. "This is our home now. We do not want to leave it. Besides, things are calmer now. Shouldn't you wait until your brother is doing better?"

It was the first time anyone had called Nitu my brother. He did call me didi, the familial term for "sister," but hearing it from Mashi's mouth had a different ring to it. The corners of my mouth crinkled as I reached out and grabbed his left hand.

He gripped my hand tightly. "Ma, we have to go back to Calcutta. There's someone there who I have to take care of."

She turned her gaze toward him expectedly. "What do you mean?"

"I have a son, Ma. He's only three and he needs me. Naina didi was taking care of him until she came here, and now Shweta didi is doing the same. I have to go back. I need to see him."

Her face turned pale. I wish that we had mentioned you earlier. Nitu and I talked about showing her pictures, but we never got around to it. She was so hurt that we had hidden you from her. Nitu still wasn't sure how much he wanted her to be in his life, and especially in yours. He never told me if that was the only reason. There are so many possibilities. He wasn't sure what kind of relationship he and Mashi would build. He wasn't sure if he wanted to let her be part of your life. Would she even leave East Africa to come and meet you? I'm certain that all of those things and more went through his head when he made that decision.

"You didn't tell me that you have a son," Mashi whispered. "You came all the way here, have been here all this time, but you couldn't tell me that?"

"I'm sorry. When I got here, I didn't know what I would find, and I didn't want to add Nikhil into that equation. This needed to be about you and me. But then I was injured, and it's never felt like the right time to tell you since then. I didn't know how."

I glanced back and forth between them. Tears were forming in Mashi's eyes, so I decided to give them a moment alone. That was my excuse anyway. I tried to release Nitu's hand, but he held on tightly. *He wants me to stay.* I was surprised, and I didn't understand why. I fidgeted in my seat uncomfortably.

Mashi gave us a slow nod, then stood, and walked out of the room. We watched her in silence. When the door closed behind her, I let out a long sigh. "That could have gone better."

"There has to be some consequence...for what she did."

"I guess so. It's still hard to see her in pain."

With a deep breath, Nitu released my hand. "I wasn't trying to punish her. I was trying to do what was best for Nikhil, and for me." He paused and sighed. "Let's get some sleep. I'm tired, and I'd rather deal with this in the morning."

I exited the room quickly and went upstairs to the room that Mashi had given me for my stay. I turned the pages in my book for the next half hour, but I kept returning to a single image. I could see it there in my imagination, as if it were real. You were sitting on Mashi's lap with Nitu and me at the kitchen table while you ate a soft-boiled egg. Under different circumstances, I would have loved to make that image a reality.

****

June, 2045 – Your question

This morning you came by the house alone. I was out buying groceries, so Dev spoke to you before I returned. After some small talk, you asked him what we knew about your birth parents. Just like that.

When we first told you that you were adopted, you didn't say much. Now, twenty-three years later, you've finally decided to ask those questions. I have always hoped that you hadn't asked because you thought Dev and I were all the parents you needed, but I know there is more to it than that. I'm guessing that you asked about it now because of your impending fatherhood. Becoming a parent makes you examine your life—past and present, as well as plans for the future—in ways you never imagined you would before a child was added to that picture.

Your father asked you to wait for me to be there so that we could to talk to you together. So my sprint continues. I hope that you aren't angry once you've read this. We had good intentions, but we've kept this story from you for too long.

****

June, 2017 – Nitu's condition

I lingered in bed the morning after Nitu and I told Mashi about our plans to leave. I didn't want to face the icy atmosphere that I was expecting downstairs. I took a leisurely shower and read more of my book. I even gave myself a pep talk. *Relax. Roll with the punches. Repeat.*

My efforts were in vain. I kept returning to Mashi's reaction. I wasn't sure if I should bring up the UN evacuation to try to convince them to leave, or let her wallow in the knowledge that we'd hidden you, her only grandson.

Even if I had the courage to try again to convince her, I would be compromising Faisal's trust if I told them about the UN. That information had been kept quiet for a reason. I was lucky that he trusted me enough to tell me, but how else could I possibly convince them? I wasn't even sure if it would work, but that was my only shot.

I peeked under the shade at the corner of the large bay window in my room, careful to keep most of my head below the windowsill. We kept the heavy drapes drawn in all of the rooms as a protection against potential attacks, and my body yearned for the sun. I'd hardly been outside since I arrived in Taisoun and the living room skylight had long since lost its novelty. My only exposure was on the short walks between the house and the car, and the car and my destination.

The sun was ablaze over Om Tais, and I could see the faraway glint of the confluence point of the two Naifas. I thought about the day Faisal and I visited the site. A few short months ago, Mashi and

Nitu weren't even a part of my life. My thoughts drifted to my mom. I was still clueless about how she was taking all of this. My dad told me in an e-mail that he was trying to help keep her calm, but if Mashi wanted to mend the distance, then she would have to make a trip to see her. As an aside, I can't tell you how many times I have explained this to Mashi in the past twenty-five years, but somehow it has never sunk in.

****

Everything changed again that day.

I was still meandering around my room when I heard a loud crash downstairs. Intuition told me it was Nitu. I charged downstairs full tilt in my bathrobe.

By the time I reached his room, Mashi was already trying to help him up onto the bed. He was sprawled out on the floor with his spine against the bed and his legs lying flat in front of him. He was obviously dazed, but he looked fine otherwise. I let out a sigh of relief and joined Mashi on the floor. Together, we supported his arms and lifted him up onto the bed.

"Are you all right?" I asked him once he looked like he was resituated.

He gave me a look, one that harbored so much grief, pain, and angst. I'll never forget it, no matter how much I wish I could.

Mashi shook her head at me, and I could tell what she was trying to say. She had already tried all of that. For the moment, Nitu was inconsolable. We walked out of the room together, leaving him to brood on his own.

When we were safely out of his earshot, Mashi put her arm around me. "I'm sorry, Naina."

I nodded, and she released my shoulders. We each took a seat at the kitchen table. The table was already set with toast and three omelets, along with coffee mugs and some fresh jam and honey. I poured us each a cup of coffee, and we proceeded to breakfast in silence. I was halfway through my omelet when I finally gathered the courage to ask her what happened. "Did you see him fall? What happened?"

She leaned back in her chair and sighed. "No, I didn't see it. I was about to take some breakfast in to him when I thought I would see if he wanted coffee or tea. I was in front of the door when I heard the crash." Her expression grew ever more pained. "I think he was trying to get to the bathroom on his own. I moved his wheelchair to the side yesterday when I took him the dinner tray. I can't believe I forgot to move it back. My guess is he was reaching for it." She shrugged. "Or maybe he was just trying to walk to breakfast. I don't know. Either way, he's finally realized what the doctor told us might happen."

I remember looking at her in complete bewilderment. The previous fears that I had so aptly squashed surfaced as I waited for her to explain.

"I'm sorry I didn't tell you about it, Naina. The doctor said that, even with the surgeries, he might never walk again."

I felt my blood pressure rising. Before I could muster a response, Mashi spoke again.

"He said it would depend on Nitu's initial response to physiotherapy. And Nitu doesn't seem interested in going to physiotherapy." Her voice was cracking now. "But," she paused, looking up at me with a wistful bit of hope, "maybe he just misses his son?"

I thought of the number of times he had asked me about you. Even then, I knew there was something deeply wrong. I had no answers for her, so I made a feeble attempt to change the subject. "Where's Tareq?"

"He left for the office early this morning."

"Oh, I see." I focused on my plate and feigned intense concentration as I cut my food up into small bits.

The sound of our knives and forks was the only noise in the otherwise silent house until the phone rang five minutes later. Mashi picked it up and started into an enthusiastic bit of Arabic that I couldn't comprehend. While she was on the phone, I took the opportunity to go into the room to speak to Nitu.

I peeked in from the doorway. He focused his gaze on the ceiling, and I could read a mix of anger and pain in his expression. I knocked softly and he answered, "Come in."

I shut the door behind me and took a seat in the chair next to the bed. "What's going on with you, Nitu?" I whispered. "I can tell there's something wrong. There's more to this than you've told us, isn't there?"

"How did you know?"

I blinked rapidly. "I don't know. You're supposed to be my brother aren't you? I guess I just knew." I shrugged. "You've barely asked about Nikhil, but I know you must miss him like crazy. I thought maybe you were calling them directly, but Shweta hasn't heard from you much either. And you don't want to start physical therapy."

"You're right. There is something else." He adjusted his position on the bed to sit up. "When they did the surgery on my spinal cord, they did some other tests, found something else."

My heart had already begun to race. *What could they have found that would make him give up this way?* He was only twenty-five. He had his whole life ahead of him. "Nitu, just tell me what it is. It's going to be okay."

He leaned his head into the pillow behind him. I watched him fight the three scattered tears that rolled down his cheeks. "Naina didi, it isn't. What they found—it's bad. I'm dying."

Sometimes I have nightmares about that moment. I felt as if someone had dropped ten thousand pounds onto my shoulders. I knew that something wasn't right with Nitu, but I had never imagined something that dire. His words were so final.

I found myself unable to speak for a few seconds. "What did they find?"

"I have stage-four lung cancer. A bronchogenic carcinoma. The doctor said it's aggressive." His gaze flitted around the room. "I've been feeling off for ages, but I didn't think it was anything so serious. We didn't have money, so I didn't get myself checked out before." He swallowed loudly. "Now there's nothing left to do. It's already metastasized to my spine and my lymph nodes." He released a shuddering sigh. "I guess my aching back wasn't because of that old injury after all."

I searched my mind for anything I could say. *There has to be something we can do.* "You mean there's really nothing? What about chemo? Or radiation? More surgery? Something?"

"There are things we could try, but I'm so far along now that it might only buy me a little time, not cure me. I waited too long, and all of that stuff, chemo and radiation, it would be really hard on my body anyway. I don't want to feel any worse than I already do, and I don't want to spend the time I have left in the hospital."

"But what if it helped you live longer? What if it gave you more time?"

"I've already played it all out in my head. My chances are so low. And the doctor said it would only buy me a little more time at this point." Nitu's voice cracked. "I want my son to still be able to recognize me during my last days…I don't want to be so sick that I can barely speak to him."

The words caught in my throat. Chemo and radiation would certainly make him feel worse, and he seemed so sure. I opened my mouth and shut it twice to stop myself from saying that the doctors could make it all better, that we'd find one who could. Instead, I asked, "So this has nothing to do with your accident?"

He shook his head. "No. If all of this was just because of my injuries, I could recover. I might not be able to walk again, as you just saw, but I would be able to try. But with cancer in my spine, in my bones, it's impossible."

I nodded slowly. "Why didn't you say anything?"

"I didn't want it to be real. Telling you—that makes it so final. Now it's real."

"Why didn't the doctors say anything to us?" My mind cycled through every interaction we'd had in the hospital.

"I asked them not to. Told them that I would tell all of you in my own time. I just needed to wrap my head around it first."

"I see." I guess I also was trying to wrap my head around it because then I just blurted out, "But, but you don't even smoke! Wait, do you?"

Nitu sighed and shook his head. "Not really since Nikhil was born, maybe a cigarette every now and then during a stressful day at work, but it's not a habit. But I did smoke a lot when I was younger. My dad smoked a lot too."

I glanced at the doorway and thought of Mashi in the kitchen. She was probably getting ready for work since I could no longer hear her on the phone. "When are you going to tell your mom?"

"I don't know."

Nitu and I sat quietly for the next few moments before I stood up. "Why don't I get you set up with a movie in the living room? One of the nurse's assistant will be here in an hour to help you with the shower." I asked. I needed to feel as if I could do something useful, albeit minor.

He nodded.

I wiped my palms on my jeans and steadied myself enough to help him into his wheelchair. We moved into the living room and I set him next to the living room couch.

"How long do you have?" The words would barely form, but I had to hear the answer.

"Maybe three or four months, five or six if I'm lucky."

"How soon are you going to…?" I looked down at the floor. I remember just staring at the pattern on the carpet. "When will you become symptomatic?"

"The doctor said probably a month, maybe closer to two because I'm young and in decent health besides the advanced, aggressive cancer. That's exactly what he said. Can you believe that?"

I did the calculation quickly. We would be home within a week. So you could start to notice that he was sick within a few weeks at the earliest. My heart sank even further when I thought of your reaction. You'd been missing your Baba for weeks and would have him return to you only to notice that he was sick. And when he was gone, who was going to take care of you? What were we going to do? A thought occurred to me, but I kept it to myself.

I felt another ten thousand pounds hovering above my shoulders again. I handed him the remote for Tareq's video drive which contained over a hundred movies, and made a hurried excuse. When I reached my room upstairs, I collapsed onto my bed with my chest heaving just as the metaphorical weight crashed into me.

****

Half an hour later, I dragged myself downstairs to check on Nitu. He waved me off, deeply engrossed in some movie he was watching. I breathed a sigh of relief. I didn't want to interact with anyone. I just wanted to wallow in my room, so I hid in there until Mashi left for work fifteen minutes later. More than anything, I didn't want to face her. *He has to tell her before we leave.* I remember being so sure that I would convince him to do so. *But how?*

From my perch in bed, I stared at the ceiling and attempted to process what had happened. I had only just found him, so how could I lose him again so soon? And what would happen to you? I knew nothing about your birth mother. Did he even have any contact with her? Would she step up to take care of you?

I glanced at the clock and decided that I couldn't wait any longer to wake Dev up. It was Sunday, so while it was a workday in East Africa, it was the weekend at home. That didn't matter. Not with what Nitu had just said. The phone rang three times before he picked up and we switched to video chat.

"Hi, my dear. How are you?" He yawned and stretched on screen.

I wanted him to be there with me—the feeling of his arms around me with my face buried against his chest. Dev couldn't protect me from this, but I knew that he would still try. I took a deep breath and tried to hold it together. "Not, not so good, babe. I, er, I-I'm sorry to wake you."

His sleepiness fell away in an instant as he scrambled for the TV remote. "What's wrong? Naina, what happened? I haven't seen the news yet. Did something—?"

"No, it's not that. Th-the political situation seems to be okay right now." I didn't mention that the UN was evacuating Faisal. I didn't want to add to what I was about to unload on him. "But it's Nitu…he, he's not going to get better."

"What are you talking about, babe? You said that he's at home now. I thought he was doing better."

"He looks better, but he finally told me what the doctors said to him."

Dev tilted his head to the side as he studied my image on his screen. He took a deep breath and frowned a little, and I immediately knew he could tell how much I needed him. I could feel him reaching out to me, wanting to hug me, wanting to hold me. "What did the doctors say?"

"When they operated on him they found a tumor. They found cancer. He has stage-four lung cancer and it's aggressive," my voice cracked and I paused to swallow, trying to stop the tears I could feel forming. "And it's metastasized to his spine, and spread to his bones. It's bad, very bad, and, and he has such a low chance of survival that…that he's declining treatment. Dev, he's going to die." The words were so final once I'd said them aloud that I understood why Nitu had kept it from me. Saying it aloud made it real. It shouldn't have been real.

The color of Dev's face turned ashen. "I'm so sorry, babe. I'm going to come get you."

Those words dissolved my last defenses, and I could no longer hold my emotions in check. A moment later, I was sobbing. I told him everything, about all of the reasons why he couldn't come to East Africa. I told him that we were leaving as soon as possible; that Faisal was finally being evacuated as well; and that I was scared for you now that Nitu was going to die. What would happen to you?

I'm not sure how long I talked. I only remember that he listened quietly. When the frequency of my sobs lessened, he spoke up again. "You should ask him."

"Ask him? You mean Nitu? Ask him what?"

"Ask him about Nikhil's mother. Ask him about what he wants for Nikhil."

I took a deep breath. I still hadn't mentioned my idea. "You're right, but there's something that I wanted to talk to you about."

Dev gave me a comforting smile. I looked at him and my heart melted. Just for a moment, Nitu wasn't dying. He had never been injured. We weren't stuck in a wonderful country that had been pushed to the brink.

"You want to adopt him, don't you?" he asked. He knew me so well, even at the beginning.

I nodded as I tried to glean his thoughts from the hazy image. In person, I would have been able to read every microexpression on his face, but the camera had its deficiencies and all I could do was wait for his response. When he remained silent, I pressed him. "What do you think?"

"I mean, well, I didn't expect us to have a child quite this soon, but Nikhil is family. If that's what Nitu wants, and that's what you want, then of course we'll adopt him. He seems like an amazing kid."

"Thank you." My eyes were tearing again. "You're amazing, you know that?"

"I know. But you need to talk to Nitu first, okay?"

"I will."

"And send me your ticket info. I'm going to be counting the minutes until you both get out of East Africa, and I want to track your flight."

"Okay." I looked at his face and sighed. "I miss you, but I guess I can let you get some sleep now."

"I miss you too. I'll call you in a couple of hours okay?"

"Sure. I love you, Dev."

"I love you too."

****

I shut my eyes and gathered my courage to ask Nitu about your mother. *There must be a reason he never talks about her.* Those questions repeated in my mind. I counted to ten and forced myself to get off the couch.

He was sitting in his wheelchair by the window and peeking out behind the heavy curtains as I had done earlier that day. A stream of sunlight had descended toward the floor like the trickle of light I was wishing for at the end of this tunnel. The glare from the reflection made my eyes wince.

Nitu didn't hear me come in so I watched quietly for a second. When he showed no signs of stirring, I announced myself. "Nitu? We need to talk."

He wheeled himself around, bumping the chair against the wall a few times. "I'll never get used to this. But then I won't have to," he exclaimed.

I sighed in exasperation and tried to stop my eyes from reflexively rolling. "Not funny."

"Too soon?" he asked.

"You think? Give me at least a day to adjust before you start that," I said as I went around to the back of his chair.

"I don't know. A day is a long time for someone with my prognosis, Naina. It's like dog years. A day for you is seven for me. Why do you think I'm reading that book you got me so quickly?"

I shook my head and pushed his chair out into the living room. There was a skylight mounted on the ceiling in that room—the only source of natural light in the house that wasn't blocked off with heavy curtains. Since no one could see through the skylight from the street, there was nothing dangerous about leaving it uncovered. "I know it's not the same as being outside," I said. "At least it's natural light that you don't have to hide from." I settled onto the couch once again and built up my nerve to ask the only question on my mind for which I could get an immediate answer. "Are you going to tell Nikhil's mother?"

I watched him shift uncomfortably in the wheelchair. When he didn't say anything, I pushed on. "You know that what you told me this morning changes everything. And I know you don't like to talk about her. I wouldn't normally push, but you need to tell me about her now. You said that she left you. Who is she? Do you want her to take care of Nikhil…after, aft—" My voice caught and I couldn't will myself to continue. It was all too fresh.

"I don't even know where she is," Nitu answered. "The last time I saw her was when she came to drop him off."

The idea Dev and I had talked about—adopting you—recurred in my mind. I wanted to broach the topic, but I was too scared. What if he said no? What if he said that he had other plans?

I imagined you there in Mashi's living room with us. Sitting on my lap and wrestling free to play on the floor. You would have distracted us completely. There's no way that we could have had a serious conversation.

"Have you thought about what you want? For Nikhil?" I asked.

Nitu shook his head. "Not really," he sighed. "I guess I'll need to talk to her. Or at least try to find her. We never got divorced."

My eyes widened. "You're married? You didn't tell me that."

"Nandani and I—we were both just nineteen. We were being crazy."

"Do you miss her?"

A faraway look passed across his face. "Sometimes. In the mornings, sometimes I roll over and think that she's there. You know, just sleeping the way we used to. The rest of it has kind of faded away, but that habit stuck around. I just roll over to put my arm around her, but then I notice that she's not there." He shrugged again. "It's not as painful as it used to be. A little lonely, but not so bad. It's been worse here without Nikhil around. He makes me forget about most of it."

"What happened between the two of you?"

"I knew Nandani was unhappy. I kept planning to try to talk about why. I'd come home from work exhausted and put it off until the next day. And then the next. And the next. That's how it kept going." Nitu's eyes moved to the floor. "So I never asked her."

"She never said anything? You didn't have any fights?"

He kept his eyes firmly planted on the floor. "Sometimes, but not that often. Not as much as I remember my parents fighting."

I could tell there was more. Even before, when he hac broached the subject, I could tell. This time I didn't let his reluctanc stop me. "What kind of fights?"

"I don't know. Mostly about money." He met my gaze for a moment. "There was never enough. She wanted new saris, jewelry, new furniture. Stuff that I didn't think was important. Stuff that I didn't have the money to buy for her."

"Did she grow up in a wealthy family?"

"Not really, but she did grow up wealthier than I did."

Knowing what I knew about how he grew up, that didn't surprise me. I kept my reaction minimal, but looked at him intently, clearly indicating that I wanted to hear more. When he didn't say anything, I spoke up again. "How did you meet her?"

The memory brought a wistful smile to his face. "Her father owned this store down the street from our house. I saw her loads of times growing up. I would take the longer route home so that I could walk by their place. I just wanted to get a look at Nandani."

Straight out of a Hindi movie. I couldn't help but think it. *Too bad it didn't end like one.* "That's a sweet story." I reached out and squeezed his hand.

"Eventually, I worked up the nerve to actually talk to her. At first, she couldn't stand me, but after a while, I convinced her to go out with me. We snuck out together a bunch of times."

Nitu blinked a few times, and I could tell the end of the story was coming.

"We spent a, a night together when she was supposed to be at some friend's place. When she realized she was pregnant, I spoke to her father. We were married a month later."

"Nikhil was the reason that you got married? But I thought—" I did the math in my head. Was Nitu really only talking about something that had happened less than four years ago? But Nitu was twenty-five, and the way he spoke of it made it seem as if it had to be more distant than your birth, and something painful that he experienced.

He shook his head. "No, it wasn't Nikhil."

I remember feeling as if I'd been struck dumbfounded. "What happened?" I whispered.

"We had the baby and two weeks later she died. She was a preemie, and we knew that she would have to fight. There was this procedure—it was risky but the doctors said that it might cure her. I don't remember all of the medical stuff. If the surgery went well, she would have had a normal life. But if it didn't, they said that she could die." His chest was heaving now. "We couldn't afford the surgery, and I was scared. Nandani wanted to go ahead with it, so we scraped it together somehow. She died anyway. My little Shanta. They couldn't save her." He stopped and closed his eyes, unable to continue without taking a deep breath. "I think we might have been happy, if she'd survived."

Nitu's chest shook as I bridged the distance to the wheelchair and put my arms around him. *Did I push him too hard?* I remember asking myself why I had to bring up such a difficult subject, as if he didn't have enough pain to deal with already. What had gotten into me?

****

When I recall that conversation, I've often felt guilty for pressing Nitu too hard on why his marriage failed. Yet, if I hadn't, I would never have known that you had another sister, even though she died shortly after birth. Nitu never showed me a picture or mentioned Shanta again, but after Dev and I took you home with us, I would wonder if she had looked like you. My hope is that her spirit watches over you, especially as you take in everything that I'm telling you now.

****

June, 2017 – Our departure

The next couple of days felt like an eternity. Mashi walked around the house with minimal interaction with either Nitu or me. We danced around every subject except for our upcoming departure. None of it made sense to me. Why would us leaving be a surprise for her? Even if we hadn't told her about you, we had every reason to leave. Plus, with you in the picture, that should have made it even clearer.

When I reflect on the situation, I think she was most upset with us because we didn't tell her about you at the beginning. Nitu tried to explain it a number of times. He wanted her to focus on the two of them to start, rather than her desire to meet her grandson. Whether they were true or not, his explanations remained unconvincing to Mashi. We never talked about it, not really. He tried to justify it, and I did my best to listen. I wish Nitu and I had been able to talk about so many things. I wasn't lucky enough to have him around for very long, but I treasure the gift that he gave me every time I look at you.

During those last few days in Om Tais, I even got to know Tareq better. We finally found some common ground with our shared love of *Star Wars*. The formality around our relationship began to fall away as we griped about characters like Jar Jar Binks and the Ewoks. At some point, I realized that he was a kind, good-hearted man who adored Mashi. When I watched the two of them together, I could understand why she didn't stay with Nitu's father, at least based on the relationship she had described to me. I still couldn't justify why she could disappear without a word and leave her son, but that insight helped me get past some of the bad blood. The relationship that I saw between her and Tareq even reminded me of my parents, and I wished that my mom could see it. Maybe it would make the situation easier for her to understand, and I still wonder if it would. Aspects of each relationship became integral elements that I wanted for Dev and me in twenty years. We've had our problems here and there, but we've been lucky to have those elements in our relationship.

In spite of my fears about remaining in East Africa, I was sad to leave as our last days dragged by. I missed you and Dev like crazy, but Taisoun had gained a special place in my heart. My second trip had lacked the exploration of the first, but the pulse of the city still welcomed me with open arms. Since the revolution, the government's platform has been rocky. I can only hope that for the average East African, change brings with it the promise of a better life.

****

Before I knew it, Friday rolled around—the day we were supposed to leave. Faisal came by to pick us up in another armored car, and the two of us helped Nitu into the car along with his wheelchair. Mashi was crying as she hugged him goodbye. We were about to shut the door when I saw Tareq nudge her to get into the car as well.

"Would it be all right if I rode there with you?" she asked Faisal.

"Of course," he agreed. "You can both hop in. I'll drop you off afterward."

The two of them joined us and we drove off. The mood remained overwhelmingly somber despite any attempts at light conversation. I noticed Mashi whispering something to Nitu, but I couldn't hear what they were saying. It struck me that I had no idea if he had told her about the cancer. I considered telling her myself, but it wasn't my place. *It might make a difference. Would Mashi come with us if she knew that he only had a few months left?* I still didn't understand why Nitu hadn't asked her that himself. Whenever I brought it up, he'd remained overwhelmingly silent. Perhaps he hadn't really forgiven her. Perhaps he was worried about the implications. If Mashi came with us to India, then she would inevitably find out about his illness. Would she want to become your guardian? Is that what he wanted? How would she react to his absent wife? Nitu shouldn't have cared what Mashi thought of that—after all, she had abandoned him—but I know that he did. It was the same reason that he worried about what she would think of him for leaving you in someone else's care to come to East Africa. He sought her approval the way a child seeks validation from their parents, and at the same time, a part of him wanted to show her that his life had been just fine without her, that he had everything he wanted, even if it wasn't the truth.

We reached the airport and the somber goodbyes began again. I gave Mashi a huge hug and wished that I could have provided her with more comfort. Whatever she had done in her past, she had been good to us in the present. I didn't truly understand how she felt, saying goodbye to her son, until the day we dropped you off at university. Upon our return, the house felt suddenly empty, even with the knowledge that you would be returning for your first break in a few weeks. Our departure from East Africa was much more final, so I'm sure that her pain far engulfed my own. She teared up, and I wanted to join her, but the waterworks eluded me. Sadness, however, remained firmly within my grasp. In about a month, Mashi had gone from being a distant stranger who was related to me to a real member of my family.

My cheeks flushed red with disappointment as I waited for Nitu to tell her the truth about his condition. Even at that last minute, I wanted him to do the right thing. I can't help but think that she knew something was wrong. There was something in her demeanor that told me, even if she wasn't ready to acknowledge it to herself. She was more withdrawn than a mother who expected her son to visit again soon. The look on her face made my heart go out to her. At the very least, she knew he had withheld pieces of the truth.

We exchanged pleasantries with Tareq, and before we went inside, I gave Faisal a hug as well. "Thank you so much for everything," I whispered in his ear. "When do you leave?"

"Tomorrow," he said. From the smile on his face, I could tell that his mind had already departed to be with a young woman who would be joining him in Geneva.

"You'll be with Arya soon. Let me know when you set a date. We're going to be there."

He nodded. "Take care of yourself, okay? And send me your wedding invite via e-mail. I'll let you know where to mail it when we get settled."

"Will do. And thank you again."

Nitu tugged at my arm. "We need to get going," he said. "Something tells me it'll take a hell of a long time for me to get through security." He motioned toward the line that was getting longer by the minute.

Without any further fanfare, the two of us headed to the immigration lines. Once we passed through, I turned around and waved at Mashi. I could see her in the distance; she'd waited to get one last glimpse of us. Nitu glanced her way for a second, but I stood there much longer. I wanted to make up for his aloof behavior. It was obvious that he didn't know how to express his feelings to Mashi, at least not without telling her the truth. He was struggling to hold it together, and I didn't want to set off his emotions, just help Mashi to see that we loved her.

I can't imagine what he was going through. After nineteen years, he had found his mother only to discover that he wouldn't live long enough to see her again.

****

July, 2017 – Return to Calcutta

Our time in Calcutta before Nitu passed was a contradiction in every sense. Each day with him was a gift, but at the same time, almost a curse. I was exhausted every moment of the day—from taking care of him and constantly putting on a brave face for you and Nitu. I could never have imagined the toll that waiting for the end, waiting for the worst would place on my psyche. Time crept by because I was already mourning Nitu's death before he was even gone. Every moment I spent as a caregiver was a living contradiction—sometimes I felt as if it would be a relief, that the agony would be over when he was gone. Yet I treasured every moment, clung to them with everything I had. Some days, I thought that he was fine—that I would wake up from the nightmare to find that he wasn't sick and everything would be as it should be. Other days, I saw symptoms when they weren't even there. I worried that each evening when I said good night to him that he wouldn't be there to greet me in the morning. Even on the bad days, I hoped for a few more days, a few more weeks, a few more months to spend with him.

Some days I could tell he was waiting for the end, and at other times, he feared it. When he was in pain, all I wanted was for it to be over, but the next night I would wish for more time yet again. I cherish those memories, but I will never forget how painful they were for Nitu, for me, for the rest of the family, and of course, for you.

****

A few days after we arrived, Nitu started to look shakier, so I took him to see another doctor. "I'm afraid I don't have good news," the doctor said after examining Nitu.

"How much time do we have?" I asked.

"Two months or so, maybe ten weeks."

But the doctor in East Africa said that we would have three or four months? I bit down on my lip. Ten weeks. Not even three months. I thought we would have a little more time together. I couldn't accept the finality of that time frame. Nitu still didn't look that sick. How could he be dying? Before we left, I took the doctor aside and pressed him for options. Chemotherapy. Radiation. Bone marrow transplant. Anything.

He shook his head. "We're too far gone now for any of that. It would just make his last moments harder. There's nothing we can do. His best option is to be at home, not in a hospital room. We'll do our best to make him comfortable."

Those words were so hard for me to accept. I wanted to take action, to fix things, but I was powerless against his diagnosis. For Nitu's sake, I put my best face on and focused on doing what the doctor said—making him comfortable. I thought I was prepared for what I was about to see.

When he started to become symptomatic, I realized that was impossible. I knew that it was going to happen. No matter how difficult, I wanted to be present for all of it. I pushed the boundaries with my job by turning meetings into videoconferences and phone calls. When I could no longer postpone my return, I flew back to Paris for only five days. Dev and I enjoyed our time together, but part of me, of my heart, stayed in Calcutta with my cousin. The most important place I needed to be. The only place I wanted to be.

On my last day in Paris, Dev asked me when Nitu stopped being a cousin who I was trying to get to know and became a cousin who felt like my brother. I couldn't answer him. Somewhere between knocking on his door in Calcutta and our return from East Africa, we made that journey. It happened over days and days, but also in the blink of an eye. We didn't start with an instant connection, but we developed something much deeper.

****

Contrary to the doctor's prediction, Nitu lived for twelve weeks after we returned from East Africa. The three of us—Nitu, you, and I— stayed in the South City apartment. Some nights Shweta stayed with us, and other nights we were by ourselves. A hospice nurse came by twice a week to check on his pain levels. I pushed for more frequent hospice care so that we could minimize Nitu's pain, but this was already more than he could afford, and he abhorred anyone else paying for it. My parents came to stay for a while when they returned from the US, and we all crammed into the apartment. Even Dev spent a week with us. We stretched every moment of those twelve weeks to the maximum, but they still felt like nothing. The two of you became an integral part of my family. I was dreading the day I would have to take on life without Nitu. I also knew that I could no longer imagine my life without you.

One night after the two of you had gone to bed, I assembled the family and finally explained what was happening. They had all felt that something was horribly wrong—the heaviness in the apartment was so clear that it could have been perceived by a complete outsider. They just never expected that it was something so terrible. We formed a support system that took us through each day, one at a time.

His wheelchair confused you at first. You looked puzzled when he didn't follow you around or run after you as you provoked him. There were no more jaunts through the garden with you pulling on his arm. It broke my heart to watch you try to get him out of the chair. The first time it happened, he tried to explain it to you. He told you that he was sick, so he couldn't run for a while. There was more that he wanted to say, but whenever he started, it didn't make sense to you. How could it? You were only three years old. You were just so happy to have him back home.

Nitu's condition began to deteriorate in the second month. Until then, he seemed fine, except for the wheelchair. His mood had improved substantially since our return. Nothing lit up his day as much as watching you play with your Lego blocks or reading you a story while you were perched on his lap.

He spoke to Mashi every couple of days, and they seemed to be getting along well. Our conversations remained separate, so I never brought up her relationship with him.

One morning, while the three of us were sitting at the table for breakfast, I first noticed the symptoms. Nitu was holding a hot cup of tea when his wrist began to shake. I spotted it when he seemed unable to release his grip. Before I could help him, the cup crashed onto the table and the hot liquid spilled all over the place. You were on the far side of the table, so you emerged unscathed, but his forearm and hand were painful for almost a week. I dressed the wounds with aloe vera and bandaged the red, raw skin until the hospice nurse could look at it.

After that, it was hard to miss the spells. There must have been earlier warning signs that I didn't notice, but after that incident, I saw them all the time. Nitu's hands stopped being able to grip the wheels of his chair, so he couldn't push himself around. He struggled with turning the water on in the shower, and transferring from his wheelchair to a shower chair became more difficult every day. A long gash appeared on his cheek from a mistaken attempt to shave.

Each time I offered my help, he refused, and as the days passed, I gave up asking. Since he would refuse whenever asked, I stopped giving him an option. I bought new cups that came with their own straws. A few times, I helped him shave, but I couldn't disguise that as well, so I let his beard run wild. When other family was around, they chipped in as well. The little tasks helped us feel useful. We were battling an illness we knew we could not defeat.

Midway through the second month, I stopped leaving him alone with you, even when I had to run short errands. I called in favors from friends and Shweta so I could split up duties watching over him. He must have noticed, but he kept it to himself.

Those tasks also gave me a way to avoid asking him about the question burning at the back of my mind. Would Nitu consider letting Dev and me adopt you? I was terrified to bring it up. Dev was visiting when he finally convinced me to ask by reminding me of something even more frightening. What would happen if Nitu died before I ever had the courage to ask him? What would happen to you?

****

Before my courage could fail me, I went to speak to him that night. I took him out to the balcony so we could survey the view as I geared myself up. I rehearsed what I was going to say in my mind. *Dev and I would like to adopt Nitu.* Such a simple phrase, but it was so difficult to articulate. I repeated it again and again in my head beforehand. Once we were there, I could no longer remember all of the reasons I'd come up with. All of the words I'd rehearsed were gone. What had Dev and I talked about? I beat around the bush as I tried to find my footing.

"How are things with Mashi?" I asked.

Nitu shrugged. "Everything's fine. We're getting along these days."

"Do you think she'll be able to visit anytime soon?" *Before it's too late?*

"Maybe. The situation there doesn't seem to be that bad. Has she said anything to you?"

"Not really," I shook my head.

"What about your friend in Taisoun? Faisal, right?"

"Yeah. He's in Geneva now. The UN closed down their office in Taisoun, at least for now."

"Oh, I see." I could hear the uncertainty in his voice. Mashi had promised to visit as soon as things in East Africa were calmer, but she didn't know that the clock was ticking. Wouldn't it make a difference? I was sure that it would. She deserved to know, in spite of her mistakes. Most importantly, Nitu deserved to spend his last few days with his mother, especially after going through so much to see her. Even with their baggage, they loved each other, and I was fearful of how the lack of closure would impact Mashi.

Because of that, I pushed further, instead of asking about you. "Are you ever going to tell her?" I kept my voice at a whisper. That was my effort to keep judgment out of it.

"What's there to tell?" His voice was distant now, further off than it had been since our return to Calcutta.

"Don't you think that she deserves to know? Don't you want to see her again before…?"

"What? Before I die?" Nitu's tone was curt and short. "Of course I do. But why would that change anything? If she wanted to see me, then she would already be here."

She doesn't realize how little time you have left. "But she doesn't know—"

"What difference does that make?" He reached into his pocket and pulled out a pack of cigarettes. He'd tried hiding it, but he had begun smoking again after we returned to Calcutta. I cornered him into admitting it when I had smelled cigarette smoke in his room. He really had kept the habit under control after you were born. Since he didn't want to expose you to it, Nitu only smoked in his room or out on the balcony, but he no longer saw any reason to stop.

I wrinkled my nose and took a few steps back. "Why haven't you told her?" I asked him quietly. "You already know that it's real. I know you haven't accepted it fully, none of us have, but shouldn't she have the chance to say goodbye? Don't you want her to have that chance? Don't you want her to meet Nikhil while you're still alive?"

He took a long drag as a single tear rolled down his cheek. He wiped it away and stared out at the view. "Do you think she would want that?" It was his turn to whisper now. Even on the twenty-eighth floor, I could barely hear him over the echoing honks from the traffic on the street below. Then I heard it, clear as can be. "What if she wouldn't come?"

There were so many things that I ought to have said. So many things that I probably could have said to make it better. It didn't matter that I didn't share his fear. I knew that if Mashi knew how little time she had left with him, she would come. I don't know how I knew, but I just knew. So I didn't try to make it better. I put my

hand on his shoulder and cringed as he finished the cigarette. Whe
he'd discarded it safely into an ashtray, I wheeled his chair inside
After I successfully got him into bed, I went into my room and la
down next to Dev. He was flying to Delhi the next morning o
business, so he was already asleep. I squeezed myself into the corne
of the bed, pulled the covers over me, and tried to sleep.

Half an hour later, I opened my eyes. I knew what I had to do.

I padded down the hallway in my slippers and booted up m
computer to make a call. It was only eleven thirty in East Africa, so
took my chances. Mashi picked up after two rings.

"There's something that you need to know," I said to he
before I had the chance to chicken out. *Nitu is going to kill me.* "
know you were planning to see us again after things in Taisour
became calmer. I don't know if you meant for us to come back or i
you would come here." The words poured out of me. "Whateve
you meant, it doesn't matter anymore. You have to come here righ
now. There's something that Nitu didn't tell you in Taisoun."

I don't remember much else from the conversation. It took a
while for me to get the words out. To explain why Mashi had to ge
on a plane immediately. To console her when her voice started to
shake. To tell her how little time he had left. When I was done, I
could already hear Mashi throwing her things into a suitcase. She
reached Calcutta less than twenty-four hours later.

****

July, 2017 – Mashi's return

Shweta's driver took me to the airport to pick up Mashi. On our ride home, I could feel my chest heaving up and down. Mashi kept her gaze fixed in front of her without even a glance at me. At least forty-five minutes of honking went by before I could bring myself to say anything. While I didn't know what to say, I wanted to comfort her. We could be miserable together at our impending loss. What finally made me open my mouth, though, was her expression as we saw the city inching by the car.

"How long has it been?" I asked to interrupt the silence.

"What do you mean?"

"How long has it been since you were last here? In Calcutta?"

I watched her draw in a long breath. "A long, long time," she whispered. "The last time I was here, my mother was still alive."

There was a time when I would have reacted to such a statement. Why hadn't she come to Nanni's funeral? Or visited her at all after Dadu's death? Those questions would have once been at the forefront of my mind, but I dismissed them as soon as they appeared. She was here now. I held my tongue and let her continue.

"It's been so long." I could see all of the pain in her face. She'd left the city and her life as if it were nothing, only to return to watch her son die.

After a prolonged silence, she spoke again. "Did you tell him that I was here?"

I shook my head. "He'd just get mad at me for going behind his back. He wanted to see you, but he was scared that you wouldn't come. I was sure that he had to be wrong."

She sighed. "Yes, I know." Her gaze was full of gratitude. "I'm so glad that you decided to tell me. Thank you. It was the right thing to do."

"I hope he sees it that way. But you're right. It was the right thing to do."

"Has he talked to you at all? About his son? What's going to happen to him?"

My voice caught in my throat and I shifted in my seat. "Not really," I said. "I wanted to bring it up but…"

"I see." I watched her hesitate. "You know, at first, I thought that I should take care of him, but I don't exactly have the best track record as a mother in Nitu's eyes. Besides, Tareq is sixteen years older than me. It would be a lot to ask him to take on a three-year-old boy." Mashi turned her eyes toward me. "Do you think that maybe you and Dev might consider…?"

I raised my eyebrows. "Are you asking me if we would…?" The muscles in my back relaxed as she nodded. "Well, I've been thinking about it a lot, and we've talked about it. And yes, we definitely would consider it."

"You've talked about it?"

"Yes. We're both a bit apprehensive. It's earlier than we planned to have a child, and I know it would be hard, but it's what we want." I leaned forward and rubbed my neck. "I need to talk to Nitu about it. It doesn't matter what we think if he doesn't agree."

"Of course."

I made up my mind to speak to Nitu that day.

****

"There's something that I have to tell you." I stood by the door of Nitu's room. You hadn't woken up yet and Mashi was waiting in the living room. I still hadn't told him that I'd called her.

Nitu gave me a puzzled look.

"I know you told me not to, but I had to do it," I continued.

The expression on his face changed slowly as he realized what I was saying. "You called her?"

"Yes. I'm sorry. I had to. For both of you."

He sighed, and I gestured to Mashi to join me. Out of politeness, I stepped into the hallway to give them some time alone. Part of me was tempted to eavesdrop, but I resisted that time. Instead, I woke you up, and after setting you up with some toys, I moved to my computer. I alternated between spending time with you and time on my work. Two hours later, I took it upon myself to head to South City Mall and purchase all of us some lunch. Shweta met me at the mall, and together, we carried an assortment of Chinese food to the apartment.

Up to that point, speaking was kept at a minimum. We laid the food out on the dining table, and I helped Nitu join us at the table. By then, he had to lean on me completely to get into his wheelchair because his legs could no longer hold him.

Shweta set you up at the end of the table with a plate of chicken lo mein—your favorite, even now. I don't remember what we all talked about. I think Shweta shared some story about what was going on with her at work, some crazy customer at the restaurant. We had a good laugh about it, so it must have been something funny. Whatever it was, I couldn't focus on the conversation as I picked at my food. I was so nervous about the upcoming conversation with Nitu that I could barely get a morsel down.

When he finished eating, I helped Nitu into bed so that he could nap. He wasn't really able to stay up for more than two or three hours at a time anymore. Mashi went to take a nap as well in the other bedroom, and Shweta and I sat on the couch with you and watched the Disney version of *Robin Hood.* Halfway through the movie, she fell asleep next to us and you snuggled up to me. One look at you made me wonder why I was holding back. I could never let you go to an orphanage. The only thing that scared me about asking Nitu was that he might say no. But I had to do it. I had no choice.

You'd already become my family. Wherever your biological mother was, she hadn't been present since your birth. True, part of the reason I wanted to adopt you was to keep you from the orphanage, but it went beyond that. Dev and I wanted you to be our family even more so than you already were.

When we first returned to Calcutta, Nitu had tried to contact your mother. After two weeks of not hearing from her, he filed the paperwork for their divorce. It was granted quickly on the grounds of her absence.

I know this must be hard for you to hear. I don't know why she left, but whatever her reasons, they didn't have anything to do with you. I know you've already made your peace with being adopted, but I still have to stress this point. Our lives would be empty without you.

****

I heard Nitu stir an hour into the movie. I shook Shweta awake and you leaned on her while I went to check on him.

He was sitting up in bed and appeared to be deeply engrossed in one of my favorite books, *Icon* by Frederick Forsyth. It's one of those ultimate thrillers, but of course, I don't need to tell you that since you love it almost as much as I do.

"How's it going, little brother?" I asked.

"Thanks for giving me this book."

I let out a sigh of relief. No other words were required. He wasn't mad at me for calling Mashi. *I did the right thing.* "Do you need anything? Are you hungry? Thirsty? Or should I just leave you to the book?"

"I'm good."

"Okay. Want to come out and sit with everybody in a bit? Nikhil's getting antsy."

"Let me finish this chapter."

"Sure," I agreed.

"Wait."

"Yeah?"

"Naina didi, thank you."

The words passed over me like a breath of fresh air.

"I mean it," he said. "Thank you for calling her. I'm glad you did."

I beamed at him and was about to step out of the room when I realized that it was now or never. Nitu was in as good a mood as any he'd been in since we arrived in Calcutta. I couldn't delay it any further. With a deep breath, I spoke in a soft but steady tone. "There's something that I wanted to ask you."

"What is it?" Nitu slid his bookmark into place.

I took a seat at the end of the bed. "What, what do you have planned for Nikhil, after you—?"

"I don't know," he interrupted. He looked down at his hands and fiddled with his thumbs. "I, well, I haven't heard anything from his mother."

"Do you want her to be the one to take care of him?" My heart was in my throat. I tried to keep my voice steady and unrevealing.

He shrugged and shook his head. "No, but what choice do I have? I don't want to send him to an orphanage."

I reached out for his hand and took the leap. "If you don't want this, then I'll understand, but would you consider letting me and Dev adopt him? We would never want him to end up in an orphanage, and well, his mother, she hasn't exactly shown the best track record." I glanced toward the living room. "He's an amazing kid, and I love him so much. I can't imagine letting him go."

Nitu stared at me blankly, and for a moment, I thought he was going to give me a square "no." I gathered my thoughts on how I could further plead my case, but it wasn't necessary. The sides of his mouth crinkled and a smile broke out across his face. "Are you sure? You and Dev, you're not even married yet, and you'd be willing to take on a child? Naina didi, I would be so grateful if you adopted him, but I don't want you to take on something you aren't ready for. I could never allow that. You've already done so much for me, and for my mother."

"You would have done the same for me had the roles been reversed."

"Maybe. I don't know if I would have just shown up in East Africa to try to find some long-lost aunt. But you have talked to Dev about this? Are you sure that this is what you both want?"

"I won't lie to you and say that we aren't scared," I sighed. "Under different circumstances, we would have waited a few years before having a child, but things don't always go as planned. Whether we have a kid now or in four years, it will be a huge transition. We're both ready for Nikhil, if you are. Please let him be with us."

Nitu hesitated. "Let me talk to Dev first."

****

Half an hour later, I called Dev and told him what Nitu had said. "Do you think you could do that?" I asked him. "Instead of leaving for Paris, can you come back here?"

"Naina, you know that's really difficult right now. I already took a bunch of time when we went to see my parents. And did I tell you about my last flight from hell? Delay after delay, sat on the tarmac for an hour. I was stuck next to some woman trying to set me up with her very pregnant, very single daughter. I told her all about my gorgeous, funny, smart fiancée, but that didn't seem to matter. Now that little old lady is stalking me on Facebook, and she—"

"But, Dev, this is really important. It's about our future, Nikhil's future. Nitu, well he may not have much more time. I mean, I don't know how long, he might…Dev, it's all just so—"

"Hey, babe, it's okay. I get it. I do. I'm sorry. I was just trying to joke with you, lighten the mood. Of course I'll be there. I promise."

I shook my head and glared at him. "Maybe I'm just not in a joking frame of mind."

"I'm sorry. I just wanted to hear you laugh, maybe see you smile just a little. I'm seldom right, but wrong again this time, my love," Dev blew a kiss at me through the screen. "What have you guys been up to anyway? Have you done anything fun?"

I shrugged. “Nothing that you didn’t see while you were here. I haven’t told everyone that Mashi’s here yet. So basically, we’ve just seen South City Mall and the apartment, with some errands here and there.”

“What’s your apartment number again? I can’t remember and my mother wants to send you a package.”

I remember that we talked for a few more minutes. That night I tossed and turned again and again. Dev had said he would return to Calcutta as soon as he could, but I knew it would take at least a few days to make the appropriate arrangements with his business. I’d been gone for so long that I began to doubt what we had talked about. Was there something that he wasn’t telling me? Was he unsure about the decision to adopt you now?

All I wanted was for him to jump on a plane to speak to Nitu. He could explain that we were both committed to the idea. But were we? Perhaps this was his way of telling me that he wasn’t ready. I couldn’t fault him for not wanting a child yet. We weren’t even married and we’d planned to wait a few years after we did get married. But now that we’d met you, and Nitu was going to die, I wanted to take you home with us.

For a while, I dosed off. In my dreams, I saw myself visiting you at an orphanage. You ran to me and wouldn’t let go, and then you asked if I would take you away from there.

I woke up frantic in a cold sweat. It was morning, so I stumbled to my computer to lambast Dev for not getting on a plane immediately. No matter what our fears were, I knew that this was the right thing to do. While my computer was starting up, my phone buzzed. The message read, “Come to the door.”

I was surprised but curious, so I tiptoed to the door. It was early, and I didn’t want to wake you or Nitu. When I looked through the peephole, my heart leapt. Was I dreaming? Dev was standing outside the door with a small rolling bag and a bouquet of birds of paradise, my favorite flower. I opened the door and he wrapped his arms around me and kissed me.

"Thank you." I held his face in my hands and kissed him again.

"For what?"

"For everything. For coming so quickly. For loving me and understanding why I had to be gone through all of this."

Dev held the flowers up in front of my face. "For bringing your favorite flowers?" He smiled and shook the bouquet a bit. "I was already on my way when we spoke yesterday. I wanted to surprise you. And you never have to thank me for loving you. You loving me back is all I need."

"So how do you feel? Are you tired? No one is up yet, so you could nap for a bit if you want."

He nodded. "A nap sounds like a great idea."

After I put my flowers in a vase in the kitchen, he stashed his suitcase in the corner of my room and lay down on the bed. The sleep in my eyes had disappeared, but I cuddled up next to him anyway. Dev put his hand on my side and we both closed our eyes.

Ninety minutes later, my eyes fluttered open and I extricated myself from Dev's grasp. I could hear movement in the kitchen, so I knew that Mashi was probably up. When I entered, a grin swept across my face. She was sitting at the table there with you on her lap while she was sipping a cup of tea. You were squirming. One of your toys was on the chair next to you, but you couldn't quite reach it. I watched from the doorway as she put you down and you grabbed your toy and settled down with it on the floor.

"Morning," I said.

"Morning, Naina," Mashi said. "Did you talk to Nitu yesterday? I'm sorry I fell asleep so early. I wasn't sure if you wanted me there or not."

"We talked."

Her eyes brightened. "What did he say?"

"He said that he wants to talk to Dev about it."

"Oh, I see. Over the phone?"

"No, in person. It works out, though. Dev came back this morning." I pointed to the vase of flowers on the counter. "He brought me those, said he had already planned to fly in last night as a surprise."

"Naina, that's great! Where is he? I want to meet him."

"Of course. He's sleeping right now. You'll see him as soon as he wakes up." I helped myself to a cup of tea. "Mashi, did you already take Nitu his tea and breakfast?"

"No, not yet."

A few moments later, I was making another cup of tea when Dev stepped into the room, groggy and a bit unsteady. Mashi smiled when she saw him.

"Hello, Mashi," he said as he gave her a hug. "I'm Dev."

"Nice to finally meet you. I hope we weren't too noisy. You should get some more rest if you're still tired."

Dev shook his head. "No, that's all right. I'll just have some of that tea that you're making, Naina." He approached me and gave me a kiss on the cheek. "Good morning, wife."

"Not yet." I winked at him and gave him a peck. "But soon."

He glared at me and reached past to grab a banana from the bunch on the counter. Banana in hand, he sat down next to Mashi and munched on it. Once he'd finished it, he squatted down on the floor next to you. He whispered a bunch of stuff to you that I couldn't hear and then the two of you went into the living room to build a mini Lego house.

You were still in the process of putting it together when I pulled him away. I tapped Dev on the shoulder and we walked to Nitu's room. He was already awake and sitting up in bed reading. "Good morning," I said.

"I've been thinking about what we talked about. I know that I said that I wanted to speak to Dev about the adoption, but I don't know if we really have time. I want to designate you as Nikhil's guardian in my will."

I blinked rapidly and moved away from the door. "There's someone else here to see you," I whispered as Dev followed me into the room.

"Hi, Nitu," he said softly. "Good to see you again."

Nitu's eyes widened. "But how? How did you get here so quickly? I thought you were heading back to Paris."

"I was planning to surprise Naina by showing up here. I was already on my way when she told me about your conversation yesterday."

Nitu took a deep breath and smiled. It lit up his entire face. I hadn't seen him truly smile in days, and now he'd done it twice in twenty-four hours. "Thank you for coming. I'm glad that I could see you again. Maybe that will make up for missing your wedding."

"We didn't get to talk enough before. We'll get some quality time now."

Dev has always been able to talk to anyone about anything. It's a talent that still mystifies and eludes me. I watched as he sat down on the bed with Nitu and the two of them started talking about all kinds of things. I don't remember the details. I think they talked about Frederick Forsyth and other books that they liked. I remember something about movies. After five minutes, Dev knew more about Nitu's hobbies than I did. In five minutes together, it felt as if Nitu had opened up more to Dev than he ever had to me. I was envious until I recalled how Nitu had shared deeper, more emotional parts of his life with me. I might not know every aspect of his life, but he allowed me to see some of the most important pieces of his soul. I realized that by finally opening up to me the way that he had, and knowing how hard that was for him, it meant I had earned his trust. The second greatest gift he ever could have given me was his trust. You have always been, and always will be, the greatest gift.

I moved toward the door and tried to cherish the bittersweet moment. It hurt to look at them. It hurt to know that this would be one of the only times I would ever witness such a scene. What Nitu had said about missing our wedding, well, I hadn't thought about it before, but when I did, I felt as if I'd been stabbed in the heart.

Once I'd maneuvered my way out of the bedroom, I curled into a ball on the couch in the living room. Mashi had taken you to the kitchen, and Shweta was in the shower. I buried my face in my hands, seeking the solace that I thought only tears could bring me, but they would not come. As you know, tears tend to flow far too easily from my eyes. I've gotten better at controlling them over the years, but they come upon me more often than I would like. That day, though, try as I might, I could not summon even one.

I'm not sure when Dev and Nitu talked about adopting you. All I know is that Nitu had, as he said that morning, made his decision to make me your guardian in his will. I imagine that spending time with Dev only made him more certain that it was what we wanted.

****

The next day, Nitu called his lawyer and made the changes to his will. I signed the agreement to become your guardian and the deed was done. After that, he stopped trying to hold on. He must have been waiting to see that you would be taken care of. You were, after all, his *jan,* the center of his world.

Dev and I began to arrange for your visa. Since the guardianship was clear, the paperwork was simpler than I expected, though it still took a monstrous amount of time and energy. I was never so grateful for his family's political connections—although I hesitated to use them, they made the process so much easier.

What was awful was how you began to notice the signs. I took you into Nitu's room one day and was about to leave the two of you alone. I'm not sure why Nitu asked me to stay in the room with both of you. I don't know whether to be thankful or sad that you don't remember such a heart-wrenching conversation.

You were sitting next to him. He told you that he missed taking you to the park and that he was sorry he hadn't really been able to go anywhere. You were so little that you didn't really understand the words, but I think you understood the meaning. He explained that he hadn't been able to take you out because he was really sick. He told you that he was going to take a trip, that he was going to see his father—your grandfather—and he would tell him everything about you. He said that you wouldn't be able to see him after that, but that he would be there every single day to take care of you and to talk to you and watch you grow up.

I ducked into the shadows by the door to the en suite bathroom. All I wanted to do was curl into a ball and sob away the pain. Yet still, the tears would not come.

When I said good night to Nitu later, something was different. He was sad, but at peace in a way that I had never seen him. I know that your conversation was for him more than for you. He wanted tc make sure that, just in case you did have some memory of tha moment, you would not feel that he abandoned you. Some of tha sentiment has stayed with you over the years. Perhaps that's why when we first told you that you were adopted, it didn't faze you. We went through counseling beforehand on how to make sure that you didn't feel abandoned, but I don't think you ever felt that way Maybe somewhere in your subconscious, you do indeed remember that conversation.

****

Three days later, I went into Nitu's room with a cup of tea like usual. Mashi had taken you to the park.

Normally, he would have been up by that hour, so I spoke gently as I entered. "Good morning." I could sense something was wrong immediately. The back of my neck prickled, but I shook it off.

When there was no response, I touched his shoulder gently tc shake him awake. He didn't stir, so I shook him harder. With shaky hands, I reached for his pulse. I pulled the covers away from his neck and fumbled around. His skin was much cooler than it should have been.

I could hear my heartbeat pounding in my ears, but I was unable to find his pulse. I screamed and Dev rushed into the room as I started doing CPR. I knew there was nothing we could do, but I tried anyway. Dev pushed me out of the way and took over for me as I reached for my phone. I was supposed to call his hospice nurse, but instead I called an ambulance. Fifteen minutes later, an emergency crew rushed into the room. They tried using a defibrillator, but Nitu was already gone. Once the crew had left, I sank into the chair next to the bed. Dev wrapped his arms around me, and I fell into his chest, my whole body trembling.

****

My world was numb for the days afterward. Four days after Nitu's passing, Dev, Mashi, Shweta, her parents, my parents, and me prayed by the Ganges River. We scattered his ashes into the water, and afterward, Dev took me back to South City. We had left you with Mamta and picked you up on the way. That night, I went to bed early while Dev and my parents watched a movie with you in the living room. Mashi was in her room packing her bag. She would return to East Africa the next morning. Since the paperwork for you had already been processed, Dev, you, and I would also leave for Paris at the same time.

I couldn't stand being in the apartment any longer. I longed for a place where Nitu's presence wasn't so marked. We would miss him no matter what, and I told myself that our urgent departure was for your sake, but really, it was for mine. When I returned to that apartment two years later, I could smile at his memory, but not at that time.

That apartment is still a special place for me. You know that, given how much time you've spent there over the years. Back then, every spot spoke of loneliness. Whenever someone leaves, the house feels empty. That's normal, but this was something much worse, much more final.

So we left. We packed up everything and drove to the airport the next evening. Shweta gave me a tearful hug, followed by a similar

moment with Mashi. When it was my turn to say goodbye to Mash
I gave her a quick hug.

“I have to try to keep it together,” she whispered in my ear.
followed her eyes and saw that she was looking at you, so I release
her with a nod. She kneeled down and gave you a kiss on the cheek
When she stood up, you tugged on Dev’s hand and dragged hi
away from the check-in counters.

“Let’s not become strangers okay?” I said. “You and Tare
should come visit us in Paris, or in New York.”

“We will.”

We watched her enter the cue at immigration. Dev and I looke
on as you played with our cart. The large wheels fascinated you lik
those on your Baba’s wheelchair. We made the mistake of lettin
you ride on the cart for a few seconds, and you were hooked. It too
me ten years to break you of that habit.

Our check-in procedure was laborious because of all of ou
luggage and the visa regulations on your passport. The whol
process took more than an hour before we passed into the securit
line and boarded the plane. As soon as we found our seats, yo
dosed off quickly. We were grateful for that since it was your firs
flight. Thankfully, you never gave us too many issues with lon
flights. You’re an even more seasoned traveler now than either De
or I, so I guess we started you early.

The first few months were hard for you. I could see you loo
around from time to time, and I knew you were looking for Nitu
When memory was kind enough to take that from you, when you n
longer wandered around looking everywhere with your Lego toy
and would just settle down with Dev, that was the first time the tear
came for me. I watched it happen and felt them coming over me lik
a looming thunderstorm just about to break. I retreated to th
bedroom and, finally, the tears poured down my cheeks. Afte

months of keeping it all in, the floodgates were open. I cried myself to sleep. Before your fourth birthday, fate had taken away both of your biological parents.

The next morning, I took you to daycare at a friend's place. I spent a few hours running errands before I picked you up. When we arrived home, the two of us sat in front of the television and watched a movie. That's the first time that being your mother began to feel more routine, more like our new normal.

I still talk to Nitu sometimes, you know. Sometimes I walk around the garden and tell him about you. I'm sure he knows everything about you already—all of your achievements, even all of your flaws, however few there are. You are a good man, and that started with Nitu, your Baba. He would be so proud of you. I'm sure that he was there when you told us today that you had proposed to Kanika. He'll be there at your wedding, and I know that he'll show up to see his grandchild. Your father and I will be there too—there's nowhere else we would rather be. You and your sister are the greatest blessings of our life together.

I'm sorry that I kept this story from you for so long. You deserve to know everything. I'll answer all of your questions. I'll tell you everything I know. All I ask is that you try not to be too angry for what we kept from you. We thought it was for the best. There was no good moment to rehash all of this. Even this moment doesn't really qualify, but if I were to wait any longer, I could never forgive myself.

With all of my heart, I love you,

Mom

****

THE END

Dear reader,

Thank you so much for reading my book. Word of mouth, and as such, reviews, are critical for any author to succeed. If you enjoyed *The Confluence*, I would be very grateful if you would leave a review on Amazon. Even if it's only a line or two, it would be a *tremendous* help. I've provided links below for your convenience.

Amazon US: http://bit.ly/ConfluenceUS

Amazon UK: http://bit.ly/ConfluenceUK

Amazon Int'l: http://bit.ly/ConfluenceIntl (automatically routes to the correct store based on your location)

Also, please sign up for my mailing list here if you are interested in learning about new releases, contests, and more. http://bitly.com/1sIlG3h

Thank you in advance!

Puja Guha

Acknowledgments

Writing my acknowledgments is always a bit of a struggle. There are so many people to thank for their time and influence, all of which has culminated in my new career as a writer, and in my latest book, *The Confluence*. First, I want to thank you, the reader. Naina, Nikhil, and Nitu are three characters near and dear to my heart, and your participation in their story means the world to me. When I first thought up the idea for this book, I was hesitant about how my readers would react to a different genre. Without your support, I would still just be a lonely soul typing away hidden stories in the back row of a Development Economics lecture, rather than a real author attempting to write every idea that comes to me from my dreams and experiences.

Growing up, I was lucky enough to be inspired by the greats. I read everything from the classics by Jane Austen and Victor Hugo, to the ultimate thrillers by Frederick Forsyth and Tom Clancy. I devoured historical and contemporary dramas such as The Kite Runner and Istanbul. Without realizing it, every book has made a mark, and continues to do so. Thank you to every author who has come before me—who has taken the plunge into a career that offers little financial security simply because you had a story to tell and you could not live without telling it. Your inspiration runs through me every day when I sit down at the keyboard.

To my parents: thank you for exposing me to the magic that each of these authors creates and for encouraging me to pursue what makes me happy. I have the luxury of following the muse because of the life that you built for us, and the blood, sweat, and tears that you poured into it. You taught me how to value my efforts and to seek comfort in the impact of my work, however small or intangible.

Mom and Dad, I remain in awe of how you have balanced work, life, family, and movements around the world to create the most loving home for me to grow up and flourish in.

Taking *The Confluence* from idea to completed final draft would not have been possible without the support of a number of my family members and friends. Eric Sukumaran, thank you, as always, for reading my early drafts and pushing me to make them stronger, to make them better. The scrawl of your handwriting on my printouts is now so familiar that you are stuck with being my beta reader for life.

Leigh Owen, my editor, has been such a remarkable force in improving every aspect of the book—from the smallest grammatical edit to pieces of character development. What would I do without you? I can only say that your touch makes each of my stories infinitely stronger.

My enduring thanks and appreciation:

- To all of those who have read and edited *The Confluence* in its various pieces and drafts.
- To the Book Divas: Sandra (B Swangin) Webster, Deliah Lawrence, and K. R. Raye, fellow authors who gave me invaluable support and intelligence on the writing and publishing process.
- To Tatiana Villa Fernandez for again designing the perfect cover.
- To my dear friend Mollie Foust: we went from being colleagues to sisters in the blink of an eye. I am so grateful to have you as part of my life.
- To another dear friend and brother: Russell Saltz, you may have moved away, but we so often feel your presence at the house. Thank you for continually supporting and sitting with

me through questions, emotions, fits of anger, and even stupidity as I moved forward with my writing.

- To Gunhild Berg, Francisco Campos, Eneida Fernandes, Andres Garcia, Valeriya Goffe, Susan Hume, Leonardo Iacovone, Moses Kibirige, Austin Kilroy, Smita Kuriakose, Ganesh Rasagam, Raha Shahidsaless, Jeremy Strauss, Jaoujata Toure, and all of my other colleagues at the World Bank Group. Your support and even encouragement of my alternative schedule has been invaluable to my writing process.
- To my friends and colleagues at Oliver Wyman who have been such strong supporters of my writing. In particular, Katharina Ley Best, Vivian Merker, Chris McLaughry, Anna Epshteyn Whitney, and Danielle Thomas.
- To my family in Kuwait, and by that I mean all of the residents of Durrar Complex, both past and present, for your loving support.
- To my deputy parents who have loved me through all of my tantrums and happiest moments: Anjna Sharma, Mohan Vatsa, Amit and Ana Ghosh, Pinak and Ratna Maitra, and Dib and Shampa Maitra.
- To Sujit and Runa Bhattacharya, Santa, Prasenjit, and Tapan Guha, and the rest of my family in India for always being with me.
- To my numerous cousins and friends whom I am lucky enough to have as part of my extended family. Thank you, Sonia Bhattacharya, Pia Ghosh, David Ghosh, Aratrik Guha, Kanika Khosla, Nikhil Maitra, Nirmal Maitra, Megha Raina, Amrita Sharma, Bakul Vatsa Stenning, and Kunal Vatsa for your relentless love and support.

Finally, the person to whom I must convey the most gratitude and thanks is my husband, Brendan Collins Snow: How many days have you listened to me vent, laugh, and cry about the plot of whatever novel I'm working on, or the frustrations plaguing me in the writing process? How many times have you inspired me to keep going? Reminded me that writing is a part of who I am and that I have to be true to it no matter what? The answer to all of these questions is infinite, as is your love and encouragement. You make me a better version of myself and I love you more than anything. I couldn't do this without you.

Connect with the Author

Email: pujaguha@pujaguha.com
Follow me on Twitter: http://twitter.com/guhapuja
Friend me on Facebook: http://facebook.com/puja.guha
Google plus: https://plus.google.com/106961837703326951468
Connect with me on Goodreads:
http://www.goodreads.com/user/show/21394716-puja-guha
Connect with me on Linkedin:
http://www.linkedin.com/in/pujaguha
Webpage: www.pujaguha.com

About the Author

Puja Guha began writing in 2010 by participating in the National Novel Writing Month (NanoWriMo), when she wrote the first draft of her debut novel, Ahriman: The Spirit of Destruction. The idea for *The Confluence* struck her during a World Bank mission in Sudan. She has lived in Kuwait, Toronto, Paris, London, and several American cities, including New York, Philadelphia, San Francisco, and Washington DC. Puja is a graduate of the University of Pennsylvania with work experience in finance and health care consulting. After completing a joint master's degree in public policy from London School of Economics and Sciences Po, she is now working as an independent consultant on international development programs, primarily in Africa and South Asia. *The Confluence* is Puja's second novel.

Ahriman: The Spirit of Destruction
by Puja Guha

"Like Grisham and Clancy... this title shines among the genre simply though superb storytelling." -The US Review of Books

Espionage. Assassins. Middle East.

When the CIA intercepts intelligence on a terrorist attack in Kuwait, Petra Shirazi, a former field agent, comes face to face with the Ahriman, one of Iran's deadliest assassins.

It was the year when global economies continued to plummet despite analysts' predictions of a turnaround.

It was the year when the Kuwaiti National Assembly consisted of the largest Islamic contingent in more than two decades.

It was the month when the price of oil plunged to twenty dollars a barrel.

It was the month when the Emir of Kuwait dissolved the National Assembly for the thirteenth time in fifteen years.

It was the day when the head of the Islamic majority of the Assembly hired an assassin and the CIA intercepted intelligence about a new wave of terrorist attacks.

It was the day that would change the face of the Middle East forever.

It was May 15, 2021.

After a disastrous mission forces her out of the field, Petra Shirazi retires from a life of espionage to work in a research position. Three years later, her division stumbles upon a money trail that reveals a massive new wave of terrorist attacks. The money trail places her in the midst of an assassination plot that implicates the highest levels of the Kuwaiti and Iranian governments. Petra will find herself face to face with the Ahriman, a man named for the Persian spirit of destruction who is responsible for a series of bomb blasts that paralyzed the Suez Canal two years earlier. As the investigation begins to unravel, the ripple effects threaten to engulf not only the Middle East and its Western allies, but also the darkest secrets of Petra's past.

Made in the USA
San Bernardino, CA
22 February 2016